THE SILVER FLAME

After surviving an air crash, Jane was told she had been married to Colin Denyer who had lost his life in the crash—and as she had lost her memory she couldn't contradict Colin's disagreeable brother Paul. But what right had Paul to tell her, 'Don't imagine I'd be willing to step into Colin's shoes!' What made him think she wanted him to?

THE SILVER FLAME

BY
MARGARET PARGETER

MILLS & BOON LIMITED
15–16 BROOK'S MEWS
LONDON W1A 1DR

First published 1983
Australian copyright 1983
Philippine copyright 1984
This edition 1984

© Margaret Pargeter 1983

ISBN 0 263 74509 0

Set in Monophoto Times 10 on 10½ pt.
01-0284 – 58522

Made and printed in Great Britain by
Richard Clay (The Chaucer Press) Ltd,
Bungay, Suffolk

CHAPTER ONE

WHEN the plane crashed as it landed, Jane was one of the few passengers to survive. She recovered consciousness in a London hospital and had no idea where she was. Perhaps mercifully she couldn't remember a thing. She lived in a dark world lit only by a nightmarish, recurrent dream. At least it seemed like a dream to Jane. There was an air hostess requesting everyone to fasten their seatbelts and a girl sitting next to her pushed rings into her hands, ordering her to put them on.

'No!' she cried, trying to give them back.

'You must!'

The girl began screaming and the boy on her other side threw Jane a beseeching glance. 'Please, would you mind? Until I get her calmed down.'

Dismayed to be involved in such an incredible scene, Jane numbly obliged. The young man spoke jerkily, he was clearly desperate. Not unnaturally she felt sorry for him. But as she slipped the rings on her bare finger she was horrified to find something else, a handbag, dumped in her lap and the girl's hysterical voice proclaiming that she could have the lot, her husband as well!

'No!' This time Jane meant to be firm, then found she was screaming herself as the plane appeared to tilt and turn upside down.

She must still be screaming, for her throat felt raw. Someone was holding her, trying to soothe her—she recognised it as a man by the sound of his voice. It was deep and cool, like a forest pool and his hands were too strong to belong to a woman.

Perhaps she had fallen out of the plane, for she didn't

seem to be on it any more. As her breathing steadied in relief, she decided she would like to take a look at the man who was holding her. This proved difficult, but when she succeeded in opening her eyes it was to meet the intent gaze of a pair of light grey ones. Eyes which turned to silver as the man surveyed her silently and a hint of steel hardened them slightly.

'Hello,' he said quietly.

She must have screamed all her voice away, for when she opened her mouth no sound came out. Mutely she continued staring at him. He had a dark face. Like his voice, it was cool and forceful. His age tantalised her. He might be thirty-five or six, a lot older than herself, although she had no idea how old she was.

She thought he might be angry when she didn't speak, but he appeared willing to let her take her time. There was a noise outside, he turned his head as if he expected someone to enter, but the footsteps went past the door without hesitating.

Faintly curious, Jane's glance followed his. The door was white, the walls beige. She liked the curtains better, they were flowered and pretty.

'I keep dreaming I'm on a plane,' she whispered, 'and I'm not, am I?'

'No.' His grip on her shoulders eased as she managed to speak at last and he sat back. He was sitting in a chair, she saw, by the side of her bed. 'You're in hospital. You aren't badly hurt,' he assured her gently as her eyes widened apprehensively. 'You've had concussion from a blow to your head.'

'How did it happen?'

'Can't you remember?'

Frowning, she stared at him. 'All I can remember is a dreadful dream, and even this is fading.'

'The plane was no dream,' infuriatingly he hesitated, 'it crashed.'

'And . . .?'

A certain wariness entered the grey eyes watching

her. 'At this stage the details needn't concern you, you're still confused.'

While this was true it was no help. Anxiously she clutched his hand. 'I have to know something!' she cried desperately. 'I don't even know who you are!'

She didn't notice him press a bell, but a moment later a nurse came in, followed by a doctor. The man began getting to his feet; she imagined he almost sighed with relief, but she didn't want him to leave her. Tightly she held on to his hand.

'Please don't go,' she gasped, her blue eyes huge with despair.

'I'll come back this evening,' he promised, disengaging his hand.

She wanted to fling herself at him and beg him to take her with him, but her brief strength suddenly seemed exhausted and she sank helplessly against her pillows again.

The doctor immediately took charge. 'You mustn't disturb yourself, Mrs Denyer. Mr Denyer knows you must rest.'

Mrs Denyer—Mr Denyer? 'Are we married?' she asked, ignoring the doctor, never taking her eyes off the man now standing in the doorway.

'I'm your brother-in-law,' he replied grimly, before disappearing.

'My brother-in-law?' Turning from the blank space where he had been, Jane gazed wonderingly at the doctor.

He was fully aware of the question in her eyes. 'Your husband's brother, Mrs Denyer.'

'Oh,' she blinked, trying to think more quickly than she seemed able to. 'So, if I'm married, why isn't my husband with me?'

'Mr Denyer will explain when he returns this evening,' the doctor spoke gently but firmly, hiding his compassion. 'If you're a good girl you'll be home in a day or two but now you must sleep.' With a nod of satisfaction he removed his fingers from her wrist and he stood aside so that the nurse could attend her.

When Jane woke the next time she felt a lot better. Her head still ached, but otherwise she was almost free of pain. She even managed a faint smile for the doctor when he returned to check up on her and was able to take a little nourishment after he had gone. Her outward calmness mightn't be reflected inwardly, but she was determined to hide this for fear they refused to allow her to see her brother-in-law when he came.

Eagerly she watched him enter her room again. She liked his tallness and confidence, it made her feel safe. Because of this she was puzzled to find tears gathering in her eyes and running down her cheeks.

'I can't think what's wrong with me,' she gulped scrubbing desperately at the tears with tight knuckles, terrified he would ring for the nurse or go away.

Giving her a clean tissue from a pack by her bedside, he advised her curtly to use it. 'You're still suffering from shock. It's only reaction.'

He sat on the edge of the bed this time, instead of in the chair, and as her tears dried, Jane looked at him closely. Something about his face made her shiver, but she was sure it wasn't with fright.

Impulsively she dropped the tissue and caught his hand, holding it tightly, as she had done that morning. 'I wasn't sure you would come.'

He smiled slightly, his eyes remaining sober. 'Didn't I promise?'

'I was frightened they wouldn't let you in.'

He merely shrugged, as if her remark wasn't worthy of a reply, and continued to study her broodingly.

She frowned at the breadth of his shoulders without knowing why. 'You've been very kind.'

'I'm trying to be.'

Her eyes darkened as she wondered what that meant. He was very pale, as though he was under some kind of strain. He was concerned for her, of course, but she sensed it was something more than that. Frustration wrenched at her painfully. He was here alone. Had his tension anything to do with her husband? He might have been with her on the plane and been injured, as she was. He could be lying ill in this very hospital and her brother-in-law could be reluctant to tell her. If only she could remember!

'It might be kinder to tell me the truth,' she whispered huskily, believing she had managed to decipher his odd remark. 'The doctor said you would— at least, he said you would explain about my husband.'

'You don't remember him at all?'

As the grey eyes bored into her, as if trying to read her very soul, she shook her head nervously. 'I don't even feel married.'

'You have rings to prove it.'

Slowly, apprehensively, her glance fell on her left hand lying idly on the white cover. Adorning her third finger was a wedding ring and a very showy engagement ring. The engagement ring, particularly, didn't appeal to her. She was sure it wasn't the kind of ring she would normally have chosen. 'I don't like it,' she murmured unhappily.

His narrowed eyes gave the clear impression that he didn't believe she hadn't noticed the ring before. 'Jane,' he leaned nearer, his voice suddenly clipped and decisive, 'your medical team agrees that you ought to be told or you'll only lie here and worry. But there's no easy way out, and you're going to have to be brave.'

'Brave?' she repeated the word after him uncertainly.

'You haven't forgotten what that means?'

'No.'

'Then listen,' he commanded, on a harsh breath. 'I'm Paul Denyer. You were married to my youngest brother, Colin. You were married in Italy, a month ago, and Colin decided to come home. It was a million to one chance that the plane developed a fault while landing and he was killed.'

'He's dead?'

'Yes.' Paul Denyer's impassive glance searched her bewildered face. His voice was hard and cold, without emotion, but she noticed he was still pale under his tan.

Again she felt a terrible sense of frustration. 'I wish my mind wasn't so blank!' She tried to control a rising hysteria although her voice wobbled betrayingly. 'You'd think I'd be able to remember my own husband!'

'You will in time.' Paul Denyer spoke flatly, obviously doing nothing to increase her distress.

'But a plane crash!' Jane stared wildly at her brother-in-law, hating his cool detachment. 'Did you . . .' she had to pause to take a steadying breath, 'did you say we'd only been married a month?'

'According to Colin.'

Jane sighed raggedly. What did she know of either time or marriage? Surely the first month of a marriage would have a very intense effect on a girl? It couldn't be something so easily forgotten. In her case, she suddenly knew it wouldn't be. Then why—oh, dear God, why did she feel so innocent?

She could find no answer in Paul Denyer's emotionless face and asked, perhaps foolishly, 'Do you know why he married me?'

Paul Denyer's eyes glinted cynically. 'Probably because you're very young and pretty, or you will be when your bandages are off and you're back to normal again.'

This wasn't quite what she had meant, but she let it pass. It was difficult to explain that she was trying to establish something inside herself which wasn't there. A feeling of reality. Hesitantly she tried again. 'What sort of wedding did we have? Was it in London? We must have gone to Italy for our honeymoon.'

'You were married in Italy, I believe.'

Suddenly Jane felt a stirring of anger. Why didn't he talk to her instead of making her practically beg for every scrap of information? Then she tried to be fair. If her husband was dead, he must also have been this man's brother. He could still be feeling too disturbed to talk about Colin easily. Colin . . .? She repeated the name to herself without a flicker of recognition.

'Italy?' she murmured vaguely.

'Yes,' he nodded grimly. 'You met there and married, without telling anyone.'

'Not even my family?' Her eyes widened with intense apprehension. 'I must have told them!'

'According to Colin you've been an orphan for years.'

Strangely this didn't surprise her. 'I see . . .'

As her voice trailed off, he said tightly, 'The medical staff here doesn't believe your loss of memory will be permanent. When I'm gone you might believe I've been rather ruthless, but if you think about it I'm sure you'll come to agree that it might be a blessing in disguise. By the time your memory returns you will have had a chance to come to terms with Colin's death and the shock wan't be so great.'

'I feel shocked now!' Apprehension and indignation returned, swamping her. Didn't he realise what it was like to be trapped in a vacuum? It was like floating in space! She still held his hand feverishly, now her other one clutched at him. 'You say you're my husband's brother. Did he have anyone else?'

'His parents and another brother.'

Her small face grew even more strained. 'His mother must be heartbroken.'

'She's extremely upset, so's my father.'

Jane was so close, he must have felt her trembling, but he didn't try and push her away. 'How old was Colin?' she asked.

'Twenty-two.'

'Do you know how old I am?'

'Twenty-five, but you don't look it.'

Jane shrank from his coolness, her thoughts jumping

wildly without getting anywhere. 'I must be tired,' she whispered helplessly.

Politely he rose, very dark and suddenly remote. 'I'll send your nurse.'

'No, Paul!' She didn't pause to wonder why his name came more easily to her lips than Colin's. 'She'll only tell you to leave, and I want you to stay.'

'I'll return tomorrow,' quite kindly he patted her upraised cheek, 'I think you've learnt enough for one day. Just remember Colin's family intend looking after you.'

Unhappily she watched him go without making any further attempt to detain him. Wistfully she wished he had kissed her cheek instead of patting it. It might have given her a greater sense of belonging. He was dark and handsome, the nurse declared she could fall for him like a ton of bricks, but Jane was wary of his sophistication. Perhaps Colin had resembled him slightly, which would account for the way some part of her responded to his undoubted masculinity. Otherwise Paul Denyer was much too worldly ever to appeal to her.

While the nurse fussed over her, Jane tried to rid herself of the insistent notion that Paul didn't like her. It was crazy to let her imagination run riot! She couldn't believe he knew she was going to worry until he came back over the many loose ends he could have so easily explained. He might have a ruthless streak, but he couldn't be punishing her for something she didn't understand. Unless he blamed her indirectly for the death of his brother?

Throughout the night, each time she woke from restless snatches of sleep she tried to recall some aspect of her marriage, but no matter how hard she probed her mind refused to release any information. Her memory remained blank apart from the things Paul had divulged. And although she realised what he had told her must be true, she still found it difficult to believe it had anything to do with her. Italy and a secret wedding seemed like a fairytale, ending in tragedy, which she had read about as a child.

The following evening Paul came early. That afternoon her bandages had been removed, and she wondered what he would think of her without them. Her doctor had explained how they had had to cut her hair but that it would grow again. Jane knew they were right, but at the moment it seemed to be sticking up all over her head, too short to be flattering.

The nurse who was with her most had laughed when she'd been worried over it. 'It's a lovely colour, Mrs Denyer. You'll see, after I wash it for you tomorrow, it will be inclined to curl. Your skin's good too, and your eyes are a beautiful blue. If I looked half as nice, I'd think I was a film star!'

Jane wasn't inclined to believe her. It could all be part of a campaign to prevent her from getting too depressed over the loss of her husband. Thinking of Colin, she immediately felt ashamed. She ought to be counting herself lucky to be alive instead of worrying over how she looked!

She watched Paul as he spoke to the nurse who was just going out. His easy charm brought a flush to the woman's normally cool face, and she wondered if he was aware of the effect he had on people. She suspected he had, even if he didn't always take advantage of it.

'You're looking rather cross,' he said blandly, sitting down beside her. 'Your nurse assures me you're improving rapidly, but perhaps you still don't feel too well?'

She suspected he knew what was bothering her and didn't attempt to cover up. 'You're supposed to be here to see me!'

From being mildly teasing, his face changed to cold civility. 'I am here to see you!' He didn't accuse her of behaving childishly, but his tone implied it.

'I'm sorry,' instinctively Jane reached for his hand, 'I didn't mean to be selfish, but you seem to be the only person in the world whom I know.' Tearfully she hesitated. 'I must be scared of losing you, too.'

He let her fingers curl round his, but his glance was guarded. 'In another few days you'll be coming home with me, then you'll meet my parents and brother.'

She didn't reply immediately as she tried to take this in. Despite what she had just said, she wasn't sure that she was looking forward to meeting a lot of people she didn't know.' 'Why haven't they been to see me?' she hedged uncertainly.

Paul Denyer's jaw set tersely and his voice had a cutting edge to it when he spoke. 'Colin was your husband, Jane. He was also my parents' youngest son. There's been a lot to arrange.'

Flushing painfully with shame, Jane waited as he appeared to be choosing his words. Then, as if he had lost patience with such a course, he added harshly, 'Colin's funeral is scheduled provisionally for Wednesday. You've been here two weeks.'

'Two—weeks!' The sudden sickness she had felt when Paul mentioned Colin's funeral was tinged with surprise. 'Surely not?'

'You weren't unconscious all the time,' he said coldly, 'although you might imagine you were.'

'I believe you,' her trusting glance defied his anger, 'I know you wouldn't deceive me.'

'You could easily consult your doctor.'

'Yes,' her mind backtracked to her husband. 'Do I have to attend Colin's funeral?'

His eyes darkened at her obvious reluctance. 'It could be postponed.'

'No.' She shivered involuntarily and hated herself. If she could feel no grief, why couldn't she pretend? She despised herself even more for trying to explain. 'If I'd been able to remember it would be different. As it is, I'd merely feel like a stranger intruding on your family's grief.'

'My mother understands this,' Paul Denyer didn't say

he did. 'She believes it could be months before your memory returns, and Colin's funeral was actually postponed until my other brother returned from abroad.'

'Abroad?'

'On business.'

'Oh, I see.' Jane lay back on her pillows. She had thought his brother might have been in Italy trying to uncover a few facts about Colin and herself and she wasn't sure whether she was upset or relieved. It might not take much to unlock the door of her lost memory, and she wondered why she felt so apprehensive.

Paul didn't stay long, and this evening she didn't try and persuade him to. He seemed preoccupied and she realised he must have plenty on his mind, not least having to say his last farewells to a beloved young brother, whom his wife couldn't even recall!

When Paul left she gazed at the beautiful flowers and expensive hothouse fruit he had brought her with tears in her eyes. He was kind, but underneath how deep did his real kindness go? She was going to need a friend, over the next few weeks, and it frightened her to realise that although outside the hospital Paul Denyer was the only person she knew, he might not be prepared to undertake this role.

He sent word that he wouldn't be in again until the weekend, when he would come and collect her and take her to his parents' home. Despite a growing anxiety over her future, Jane was eager to leave. While the treatment she received was wonderful, the hospital was becoming more like a prison each day. She spent most of her time out of bed now, but she was growing tired of being restricted to one room.

She had been waiting for what seemed hours before Paul arrived to pick her up. It was the first time she had seen him dressed in anything else but a suit, and her eyes clung in peculiar confusion to the pair of casual black slacks and shirt that she wore. The outfit emphasised the lean toughness of his body—his shirt, the breadth of his shoulders, his pants, the powerful muscles and length of his legs.

'Good morning,' she said shyly, tensing slightly as his cool glance went over her and she realised he was aware of her interest. Unhappily she admitted his disapproval was justified. How could she even look at another man when she had just lost her husband?

'Hello, Jane.' He bent to pick up her suitcase, which contained her night things. This was all she had as her clothes had been destroyed on the plane. What she had now, Paul had bought for her and had sent in.

He looked surprised when she stood up. 'Somehow I thought you'd be taller.'

'You've only seen me in bed,' she smiled.

'How tall would you say you were?'

She wondered why her height appeared to be bothering him. 'I'm not sure,' she shrugged. 'I would say, not very.'

He went on considering her. 'My secretary didn't make a bad job of choosing that dress. The size is right, I guess it's my fault the length is wrong.'

It probably was, but she didn't intend to start grumbling. 'It doesn't matter,' she laughed. 'After this I can buy my own.'

Either her laughter or what she had said was wrong, for his face changed grimly. 'We'd better be getting on our way,' he muttered. 'Colin's parents are waiting.'

Jane sighed as she followed him out. She had a feeling he had spoken of Colin deliberately and she deeply regretted that he had thought it necessary to remind her. She was sad that she had to remind herself that she was going to a house of mourning and for the first time she wished she had had a place of her own.

Paul had a nice car, low and sporty, very fast. She felt her spirits lift a little as he helped her into it, and again without thinking she smiled at him.

'Don't do that,' he snapped.

Alarmed, she shrank from him. 'Don't do—what?'

'Smile! As if you've suddenly discovered the world is a wonderful place. Can't you damn well remember you're supposed to have just lost your husband?'

A slow trickle of tears fell on her cheeks as the contempt in his voice flicked her rawly. 'I'm sorry, Paul.'

'Sorry? Oh, come here!' With a smothered groan he drew her to him, regardless of the interested glances of passers-by. 'You'll have to forgive me. I know how difficult it must be for you. I criticise you for forgetting and do the same thing myself.'

Wearily Jane shook her head. She could have drawn from his arms, but she felt so safe she couldn't resist the temptation to cling to him. His hands touched her hair, now a cap of silky curls, and she felt his lips on her brow, softly caressing, as if he was comforting a child. Miraculously her tears dried and she snuggled against him, the feeling rushing through her anything but childlike.

'Hi!' firmly he put her from him, 'I think we'd both better remember where we are.'

'Yes.' She stared at him and confessed, an odd little catch in her voice, 'I get this urge to be close to someone.'

'You're missing Colin,' he said abruptly. 'It can't be anything else.'

'It must be,' she agreed uncertainly.

'Just as long as you don't go throwing yourself at every male who crosses your path,' he warned, half teasingly. 'If you need a shoulder to cry on, perhaps you'd better stick to mine until your memory returns. It might lead to fewer complications!'

'Thank you,' she whispered, unable to joke about it. She wondered what he would say if she were to reveal an urgent inclination to take up his offer immediately. His shoulders were broad, the arms he had wrapped round her strong, and something told her he knew how to use them. Her eyes shifted to his mouth and she guessed he had had lots of experience. In confusion she flushed and looked away, pretending to be eager to see London.

'It might jog my memory,' she said.

Streets and houses flashed by, but nothing did. She could have been anywhere in the world. 'It's hopeless!' she exclaimed.

'Give yourself time,' Paul advised, reverting to his former coldness.

'That's all I seem to have.'

'And a load of self-pity.'

'I suppose I asked for that,' she said bleakly, while wondering how his mood could swing from sympathy to harshness so swiftly.

'Where do you live?' She forced herself to break the ensuing silence eventually, as Paul made no effort to.

'My parents live at Coombe Park. It's only nine miles from the West End, but it's really like living in the country.' He glanced at her consideringly. 'I think you'll like it. The house is near the golf course and as you get better you'll be able to walk on Wimbledon Common and in Richmond Park.'

The names meant little to her, but she was grateful for the general picture he painted. His parents' home sounded very nice. 'Don't you live there too?' she asked.

'Mark and I have our own apartments in town,' he replied curtly, 'but Colin still lived at home. He hadn't got round to finding a place of his own. I imagine he would have done now, if things had been different.'

'But neither you or your brother are married.'

'What's that supposed to mean?' his eyes flicked her again. 'Both Mark and I are older and find it more convenient to be nearer the centre of things.'

Jane sighed, suddenly so curious about him she found it disturbing. 'I don't mean to pry,' she said quickly, 'it's just that I feel so terribly ignorant.'

'I notice you haven't asked about Colin's funeral,' he retorted bluntly.

Her face pale with strain, Jane turned to him. 'I know I haven't,' she whispered, 'but you surely can't believe I haven't been thinking about it? I don't expect you to understand,' she went on bitterly, as his mouth tightened, 'but I hate having to pretend to be heartbroken when I don't feel it. I think I've told you before, it seems to turn me into the worst kind of hypocrite.'

'You could be something a lot worse,' he replied cryptically, causing her eyes to darken with a mixture of anguish and horror.

Mercifully, before he could make another of the hurtful remarks which he appeared tempted to hurl at her from time to time, he turned off the main road on to a minor one and from this to a private drive and a house which she believed must belong to his parents.

It was a beautiful house, standing in its own grounds. Much too large for two people, she would have thought, but she could understand how, even after one's family had grown up and flown, it would be a wrench to leave such a place.

Paul didn't give her a chance to express her admiration, however, as he whisked her inside. 'You'll have enough time to say what you think of it later,' he snapped, clearly critical of the enchanted glow in her eyes. 'Right now you should be more concerned with the people living in it.'

It wasn't a very auspicious beginning and it made Jane wonder apprehensively what kind of reception she was about to receive. Paul's parents, though, couldn't have been nicer. It almost overwhelmed her that they welcomed her as they did.

Mary Denyer was in her sixties, her husband, John, ten years older, but even at their age, when the loss of a son weighs particularly heavily, they found strength to put their own sorrow aside for a moment to consider Jane's.

Mary wrapped her in her arms, while John patted her shoulder gently, both making it clear from the start that they understood the distressing and peculiar circumstances she found herself in, and immediately removing any anxiety she might have that she would be exposed to any kind of pressure. Mark Denyer, who hovered nearby, expressed his sympathy too, and was so pleasant to her during the following days that if she hadn't been so hurt by it, she might never have noticed Paul's increasing coldness.

John Denyer, Jane soon learned, was retired and Paul now ran the family business which, she gathered, had something to do with advertising. Mark worked in it as well, but it appeared he had no desire or aptitude for responsibility. He was quite happy to leave that to his elder brother. On taking Jane to her room, Mary Denyer had told her briefly how Colin had been spending a few months abroad after leaving university, before commencing training for the U.K. side of the business, so as eventually to leave Paul more time to concentrate on their overseas markets in which he was more interested.

'Colin and I must have met abroad.' Jane spoke to his mother hesitantly, the morning after she arrived.

They were having coffee alone together on the terrace as the late summer weather was still warm and John Denyer was keeping an appointment in town. Paul and Mark had apparently left hours ago, for there was no sign of them. Mary had wanted Jane to stay in bed, although the hospital had assured her this wasn't necessary as she was almost fully recovered, apart from her memory. When Jane had reminded her of this, Mary had given in, contenting herself with begging Jane to be careful.

Jane hadn't been sure whether to speak of Colin or not. Since she had no recollection of him whatsoever, he was a very remote figure, yet she was curious to know more about the man she had apparently loved enough to marry than Paul had told her. She felt grateful, therefore, when Mary began talking about him, thus taking the decision out of her hands.

After apologising for not coming to see Jane in hospital, Mary said tremulously, 'We loved Colin so much and had such hopes for him.'

This was when Jane pondered on how they had met. 'Paul believes it was in Italy?' she queried.

'We believe so,' Mary agreed. 'I'm afraid,' she confessed, 'it was a shock to learn that he was married. He rang Paul, you see, to say he was bringing you home, but when he was killed we were shattered. When Paul told us you'd lost your memory it seemed the last straw. For the first time in my life I found I couldn't cope.'

'I'm terribly sorry,' Jane whispered, beginning to realise, on top of everything else, just how much Paul must have had to do. She felt ashamed for having resented his absence from hospital during the past few days.

'Oh, I'm all right now, as far as that goes,' Mary said quickly, 'and I expect in time the pain will ease. You have it to face yet. It worried me a lot as to what you would do if your memory returned and you were in hospital alone, without anyone to turn to. I should have been there.'

Even though Jane still couldn't remember her husband, her heart ached with pity for his mother. 'I don't think it would have helped either of us if you had come to see me,' she said gently. 'You might only have been even more upset, and Paul saw to it that I had everything I needed. He was very kind.'

'He can be,' Mary sighed, 'but he isn't always as kind as he might be to women. That I'm his mother doesn't make me blind to his faults. He has affairs with women, but he never seems to consider the long-term advantages of marrying one of them.'

'Advantages?' Jane felt her head throb as it frequently did when she concentrated on something.

Mary smiled faintly. 'You know, a settled home and wife, possibly children. John and I are beginning to think too much of grandchildren, I suppose. That's why, after the first shock of learning Colin was married had worn off, we were so thrilled about it.'

Jane felt a sting of remorse for getting married secretly and depriving this kind woman of so much pleasure. 'I don't know why Colin and I chose to be married without telling anyone,' she said fiercely, 'but I hope there was a good reason.'

Mary mused, obviously without thinking, 'Paul ruled out the obvious one.'

'The obvious one?' Jane repeated in an uncertain whisper, feeling suddenly apprehensive again. Paul Denyer, with his superior, ice-cold intelligence, would have been unlikely to leave any stone unturned!

Now Mary looked flustered. Noticing how white Jane had gone, she clearly wished she had never said anything. 'It doesn't matter, dear,' she hedged awkwardly. 'Would you like some more coffee?'

'No,' Jane refused sharply, and though she added a thank you and an apology, she insisted, 'I think you have to tell me.'

'Well,' Mary sighed reluctantly, 'maybe I should have held my tongue, but it's not anything to get upset about. Paul was sure—that is, he merely wondered if you could be pregnant, but your doctors said that wasn't possible. They convinced him there wasn't a chance.'

CHAPTER TWO

THERE wasn't a chance! Jane stared down at her hands, surprised to find they were trembling. The hospital would merely have been taking routine precautions, especially as she must have been unconscious and unable to tell them anything herself. It was Paul's attitude that shook her. She wondered, recalling how his eyes frequently dwelt on her suspiciously, if he believed she had blackmailed his brother in some way into marrying her and was determined to find out. Paul's investigations, unlike those of a hospital's medical staff, could be dangerous.

After dinner that evening, Jane retired early. She was feeling very tired, but it wasn't only this. With the exception of Paul everyone had been kind to her, but she still had the uncomfortable feeling of being an impostor. Mrs Denyer had told her that both Paul and Mark intended staying at Coombe Park until Jane settled in, but Jane, conscious throughout the meal of Paul's narrowed gaze on her, couldn't help fearing that, in her case, something other than concern lay behind his decision to stay at home and help look after her.

During the meal, served by the butler and a maid, it was Mary and Mark who kept the conversation going. Both Paul and his father appeared preoccupied, although Jane doubted if it was over the same thing.

Mary came with her upstairs and said if Jane felt well enough the next day they might visit a nearby boutique and replenish her wardrobe.

Jane, glancing ruefully at her now very crumpled dress which was the only one she had, was reluctant to accept Mary's offer, but when she suggested washing it, Mary firmly shook her head.

'You should have some new clothes, dear, and it's not as though we're contemplating a shopping spree at such a time. No one,' she added gently, 'would understand that better than Colin.'

Jane hadn't the heart to disagree, but she hated being too poor to buy her own clothes. When her memory returned, she prayed she would discover she had enough—somewhere, to give her some degree of independence. There had been nothing in the handbag she had apparently been clutching, when she'd been thrown from the plane, apart from a few Italian lire.

Mary left her, promising that the housekeeper would be up later with some hot milk. After promising to drink it, Jane said goodnight and prepared slowly for bed. She took a shower, then dried her hair, watching it waving entrancingly about her small head without any real interest. She felt quite well but terribly lethargic. Even the smallest task seemed to take an astonishing time to complete.

When a knock came to her bedroom door, she thought it was Mrs Finn with her milk. In a low voice she called for her to come in. She mustn't let Mrs Denyer make the staff wait on her like this. She was sure she wasn't used to it.

It wasn't Mrs Finn who came in, it was Paul. He was carrying a tray with a cup of cocoa and some biscuits on it. 'My mother appears to imagine you need feeding up,' he said, unpleasantly.

'Thank you.' Jane decided to ignore his gibe, and she was sure it was one. 'I told her it wasn't necessary.'

'Oh,' he smiled slightly, 'she'll welcome the chance to make a fuss of someone. She always spoiled Colin.'

Did he have to be deliberately cruel? As she went white he put the tray down and bent towards her, the paleness of her face obviously provoking him to scrutinise her more closely.

She was sitting by her dressing-table. He put a finger under her chin to tilt it. 'Enchanting, aren't you? So small and fragile, you don't look the least bit tough, but I wonder . . .'

'Paul, please!' She felt a surge of hurt indignation, because his attitude bothered her. 'If you've something on your mind I wish you'd tell me.'

'Haven't you anything on yours?' he countered coolly.

'Nothing that won't keep,' she replied steadily, hating the way he so often appeared to be accusing her of duplicity.

'You do surprise me.' Again he smiled, a slightly cruel smile which wounded Jane irrationally.

'Is this why you brought me something to drink?' she exclaimed. 'To have a go at me?'

His brows rose mockingly at her outburst. 'Now I wonder why you should think that? Haven't I been good to you?'

'Yes,' she couldn't deny it, 'and I'm grateful.' Anxiously her blue eyes widened on his as she tried to make him believe it, and her soft lips trembled.

'I came to tell you something,' he said abruptly, 'not to have a go at you.'

'You've discovered something about me?' she asked eagerly. 'Apart from the fact that I'm not pregnant!' she muttered bitterly.

'Who told you that?'

'Your mother. I don't think she meant to.'

'Aren't you pleased you aren't?'

She flushed, wishing she had never mentioned it. 'It would have added to the complications, I suppose, but your parents might have been pleased.'

'It's Colin's money I came to talk about,' again he changed the subject abruptly. 'My father and I saw his solicitor today and the money he inherited from his maternal grandmother will come to you, along with some smaller sums. I've asked that it should be held back as long as possible.'

'Why?'

'Greedy little bitch, aren't you?'

Jane couldn't speak. This time there was no mistaking the level of dislike and distrust in Paul's voice. It stunned her, and she was ill equipped to deal with it.

'I don't want Colin's money.' She found her voice at last, if it sounded husky. 'I don't deny I wouldn't mind discovering I had some of my own, but I don't consider I'm entitled to his, not after being married only a few weeks. When I asked why, I meant, why are you opposed to it?'

'I'd like to be sure you deserve it.'

Something in the hardness of his eyes drove her to defy him. 'Can you legally prevent me getting anything?'

'Why, you mercenary . . .'

'Paul!' she twisted from the hands which suddenly gripped her savagely. 'I—I'm only trying to point out that I know my rights, even if I don't intend demanding them. Just to prove I'm not mercenary!'

'Your memory seems remarkably clear on some things,' he rapped, clearly unimpressed by her stammering speech, countering it with more accusations.

Jane swallowed, the movement regrettably bringing his glance to her long, slender throat. 'A lot of things are coming back, but nothing of any great importance.'

'Have you no idea why full recall remains so elusive?' he asked coldly.

'No, I haven't!' His jeering insolence set her teeth on edge. 'What I appear to recall are ordinary, fundamental facts I've probably been familiar with for years. Possibly I don't remember my marriage, or that period of my life, because it's so recent.'

'I apologise,' he shrugged derisively. 'You must be winning.'

'You imply that I am, at the moment,' she retorted unsteadily, 'but would I be right in thinking your apology holds some kind of warning?'

'Yes,' he retorted curtly. 'You're obviously above average intelligence and in a strong position. If you don't remember anything else, Jane, remember this. Take advantage of it and you'll have me to answer to!'

His voice was so hard she flinched, but managed to assure him tensely, 'I don't intend hurting anyone or taking advantage of anything.'

'Good,' he drawled. 'You wouldn't find it worth the repercussions.'

Later Jane wondered if it was because Paul had disturbed her so much that the nightmares began again. This time there were no people in her bad dreams. They were illuminated only by vivid flashes of light. She was alone, caught up in a vortex of fire, struggling desperately, trying to escape from someone whose arms of steel imprisoned her firmly.

She didn't realise it was Paul until he succeeded in getting through to her. Apprehensively she opened her eyes to find him beside her. He was holding her, soothing her, as he had done so frequently in hospital. Only she wasn't in hospital now. She was a guest in his parents' home and she doubted if they'd approve of him being here.

'Paul?' She tried to control herself sufficiently to tell him so, but she couldn't get the words out.

'Hush,' he murmured gently, and she was grateful, despite her anxiety over propriety, that he didn't immediately let her go. The panic inside her was still there.

'I had a terrible dream,' she whispered.

'I heard you.'

'Did you?' Blindly her eyes wandered from the vee of his robe, past his slightly shadowed chin, to meet his downward gaze.

He waited until her dazed eyes met his, then he

nodded while his hand smoothed the damp curls from her hot forehead. 'As a matter of fact I was warned when you left hospital about your nightmares, so I expect I was prepared.'

Jane licked her tongue over suddenly dry lips. 'I'm sorry if I woke you.'

'I wasn't asleep. I was working in the study and hadn't been long upstairs. When you began screaming I knew what was wrong and didn't want my parents disturbed.' He paused, his eyes sombre. 'They've been through enough lately.'

'I know,' she whispered, feeling a terrible sense of remorse. 'It can't be easy for any of you. I'll try not to let it happen again.'

'How long since the last one?' he asked abruptly.

'I think about five days.'

'They'll probably not disappear completely until your memory returns.'

'I wish it would,' she sighed.

'Don't we all!'

Uneasily she stirred beneath his speculative gaze, seeing in it the now familiar suspicion. 'I can't help having bad dreams,' she said defensively.

'No,' he agreed coldly. 'And until they stop I'll be here to see you through them.'

'Thank you.' Her voice trembled faintly.

He regarded her grimly for another minute, then rose. 'You need a drink.'

'No, Paul!' Frantically she grasped him, refusing to let him go. Suddenly she was terrified of being alone. 'Could you stay and hold me for a little while? she begged. 'Please!'

'If you like,' he muttered tersely.

As he sank down again on the side of the bed and pulled her to him, the tremors shaking Jane's slight body subsided. Briefly she felt calmer. 'Thank you,' she gulped.

'Don't be too grateful,' he replied curtly. 'You realise

you can't make a habit of this? When I visited you in
hospital you always tried to hang on to me.'

Jane shivered, aware both of his anger and
reluctance. He only stayed for fear she had hysterics if
he didn't. Her breath caught on a half sob. His arms
were strong, she liked their strength, but it worried her
that she might be using her nightmares as an excuse to
keep him near her. As her panic faded, she was
conscious of another emotion taking its place, but before
she could examine it Paul asked impatiently,

'Are you feeling better?'

He wasn't giving her much time! 'Yes, but I still don't
want you to go.'

'Is this a different invitation?' he drawled cynically as
Jane's clutching hands tightened.

She tried to ignore the unwelcome note in his voice.
Crushed up against him, her heart was beating too fast,
she kept her eyes closed so she wouldn't see the derision
in his. 'Don't you understand I get frightened?'

'Your heart's certainly beating like a trapped bird's,'
he allowed, pressing long fingers over it.

It began racing as he touched her bare skin.
Involuntarily she jerked back, her eyes flying open,
suspecting from his taunting expression that he had
acted deliberately. What was he trying to prove? She
stared at him uncertainly, her eyes dilated to an intense
blue before she wearily gave up.

'Will you stay?' She hated having to plead with him,
but she couldn't seem to help herself.

'Yes,' he appeared to give in, 'but you'd better lie
down. I don't enjoy being tempted by a woman with
nothing to give.'

She felt bewildered, and again it showed in her eyes
as she looked at him. 'Whatever do you mean?'

'Oh, never mind,' his shoulders lifted sardonically,
'let's just concentrate on getting you to sleep. Haven't
you some pills?'

'I've already taken two.'

'I see.' Frowning, he hesitated. 'Then if you won't let me fetch you another hot drink, I can only advise you to close your eyes and we'll see what happens.'

Guiltily, after searching his dark face for something she couldn't seem to find, Jane obeyed him. What was the use of looking for a hint of warmth and compassion when he had none for her? Yet why should he when she was virtually a stranger? It must be crazy, perhaps a part of her disability, that her senses reacted so strongly to his dark attraction. If only, she thought feverishly, she could recover her memory! She would give everything she possessed for it to happen, even if it meant she would be devastatingly aware of the loss of a beloved husband.

She sighed as Paul carefully straightened her pillows and smoothed a sheet.

'Paul?' she whispered, lifting heavy lashes to stare up at him again, trying to thank him.

'Shush!' He wasn't encouraging. 'No more talking. I know you have a lot on your mind, but it will keep.'

'Why are you always so sure?' she protested.

'Because all you want to do is ask questions,' he said relentlessly, 'and I don't know the answers. No one will until your memory returns,' he added enigmatically.

She couldn't argue with this, although his hardness hurt. Blindly she closed her eyes, for fear he should see the tears in them. He was a hard man. What he said might be true, but he didn't believe in sparing her.

Eventually she dozed, but didn't fall into a deep sleep until she had woken several times and been reassured by Paul's presence. An early dawn was creeping through the window when she woke again to find him sleeping soundly beside her. He was on top of the sheet while she was underneath it, but it had slipped to her waist. One of his arms was around her bare shoulders, his face only inches from her own. He still wore his robe, but the cord round his middle had slackened, revealing an expanse of hair-covered chest.

Taking care not to disturb him, Jane almost held her breath as her glance slid slowly over him. The strength of his features hadn't escaped her before, but, this near, she found herself studying him closely. His brows were expressive but not unruly, his lashes thick, curling sightly at the ends. As did his mouth, which in sleep was more relaxed than it usually was, the bottom lip fuller. He was breathing quietly and her fingers suddenly itched to explore the hard bones of his face, to bury themselves tightly in the darkness of his rumpled hair.

Tentatively the arm which wasn't crushed against him lifted, as if with a will of its own. Yet her movements were awkward, confirming a sudden, startling conviction that she had never been quite this close to a man before. Not in bed, anyway, in a man's arms. Flushing deeply, she reminded herself sharply that she had been married, so such thoughts were irrational. She also reminded herself, just as sharply, that Paul wasn't for her and she had no business lying here thinking about him as she was doing. She ought to be ashamed of herself and wakening him up, thanking him for staying but sending him back to his own room.

Then why did she make no attempt to do so? Curiously only her hands moved, creeping towards him. She smiled softly, half tenderly at the slight rasp of his jaw on her fingertips. The cleft in his stubborn chin beckoned, as did his sensuous lower lip. She bit her own lip unconsciously as a warm wave of something alien rushed through her.

'Enjoying yourself?'

Her face going from scarlet to white, Jane withdrew her fingers as though she'd been burnt. 'I didn't realise you were awake.'

'I'm not used to women paying me so much attention at this time of morning!'

'Because you aren't married?' she gasped, squirming helplessy against the arm which tightened to a punishing grip around her shoulders. Embarrassment threatened to consume her that he had caught her at such a vulnerable moment, but he refused to let her go.

'A man doesn't have to be married to have a woman in his bed,' he said dryly, 'but most women seem more concerned about their appearance than anything else when they wake up.'

'Are they?' she wondered aloud, not having given a thought to her own. She had been too busy studying his. 'You'd better let go of me,' she decided to beg rather than struggle. 'You can't really want to stay here.'

'You might have another nightmare,' Paul teased, without doing as she asked.

'I don't have them during the day.' As her pulse steadied a little, she looked at him suspiciously. He must know that. 'Have you been with me all night?'

His mouth twisted in a teasing smile. 'Twice I got as far as the door before you showed signs of getting restless. I decided it might be easier to stay.'

'Thank you.' Suddenly, for the first time since she had recovered consciousness in hospital, Jane felt completely relaxed. The room was quiet, the whole atmosphere soothing, Paul's breath still soft on her face. It puzzled her how she could feel so calm when he usually disturbed her so much.

She broke the silence at last. 'I mustn't get too lazy in the mornings, Paul. As soon as my memory returns and I know what I did, I must begin working again.'

'Give it time,' he said tightly.

'Your usual advice!'

'Not mine,' he replied impatiently. 'Your doctor's.'

'Well, you don't have to be so cross!' she sighed. 'I'm sorry if I upset you.'

'That's not the right word,' he muttered ironically. 'Here I am, feeling extremely comfortable and almost asleep again, and you begin talking of things guaranteed to disturb me.'

She looked at him through the screen of her lashes,

feeling suddenly disturbed herself. Strange sensations began pricking her skin as she watched his glance wandering over it. She knew a fierce desire to be even closer to him than she already was. His mouth tempted while hers tingled, although he made no attempt to kiss her. She feared, if he did, she might melt. .

'Passionate little thing, aren't you?' he jeered tauntingly.

Jane swallowed an odd constriction in her throat. 'What makes you think so?' she asked angrily, not liking his tone.

'I can sense you might be quite violent when your feelings are aroused. Are you missing Colin?'

Horrified, she sat up, forgetting how her thin nightdress concealed nothing of her figure. His question shocked her back to reality. She was sure he had asked it before, he wielded it like a weapon whenever she got too near him, but this time she couldn't forgive him for using it so ruthlessly. 'You're despicable!' she cried jerkily.

'Why?' He pulled her down again, his brows rising innocently.

She tried not to feel the impact of his hand on her arm. 'Because of what you imply . . .'

His eyes fixed on her mouth, making her quiver. 'If you aren't missing Colin then it's another man, or any man. Am I far wrong?'

'How would I know?' she faltered, quite incapable of dissecting herself as Paul appeared to be doing.

Suddenly he turned on her, thrusting her against the pillows, allowing his head to drop until his mouth crushed hers with devastating brutality. Then, as an explosion took place inside her, he as swiftly withdrew, leaving her utterly shaken.

'Does that help to explain?' He met her dazed eyes mockingly. 'I may be willing to oblige so far, but don't imagine I'd be willing to step into Colin's shoes, ever!'

She didn't try and stop him as he rolled away from

her, off the bed, out of the room, disappearing in
seconds, slamming the door. It was like switching to
cold after a hot shower. His ruthless kiss had burned
while his words froze, and she felt terribly mixed up.
She couldn't recall being kissed before so she couldn't
make comparisons, but if she responded to all men as
she did to Paul, he might be justified in hinting that she
was promiscuous. It might be no use trying to convince
him otherwise until she had proof.

She was wearing one of her new dresses the next
evening when she came down to dinner. It was silky and
plain, relying on its cut more than anything else, and
Jane had been surprised to see how well it suited her.
The trip to the boutique had been an ordeal in more
ways than one, but the difference to her appearance
proved it had been worth it.

Mark whistled. 'You're looking quite beautiful,' he
said, bringing her one of the drinks he was pouring.

Jane accepted it with a faint smile as she walked
further into the lounge. She had thought Mark alone
until she noticed Paul standing broodingly by the
window.

He raised his drink in mocking salute just before she
took a sip of hers. 'That must have set someone back
quite a packet.'

Of course he would be knowledgeable about women's
clothes. She could tell from the way his glance went so
expertly over her. Flushing a little, for she was still
unable to endure his gibes with equanimity, she retorted
defensively, 'Your mother bought it for me. We went
out today.'

'You're recovering rapidly,' he commented,

'I must be.' She tried to match his sarcasm. She
didn't reveal how weak she had felt most of the time she
had been in the boutique.

Mark interrupted, ignoring Paul. 'I don't think
you're as fit as all that. You're probably feeling
exhausted.'

'A bit,' she confessed, looking at him gratefully.

'It amazes me the lengths women will go to for new clothes,' Paul said grimly, his eyes on Jane's sweat-beaded upper lip. 'You'd crawl to the shops if you had to, wouldn't you?'

'Your mother considered it necessary.' She hated bringing his mother into it when she had been so kind, but she suddenly had an urgent desire to defend herself. Paul had obviously decided she was out for all she could get.

'What was wrong with what I supplied?'

'Nothing,' she replied uncertainly, 'but there wasn't enough. Only one dress . . .'

'Won't you sit down, Jane?' again Mark interrupted quietly, frowning at Paul. He was less aggressive than Paul, much more easygoing. As Jane sank, with almost a sigh of relief, on to a rose brocade sofa, she wondered how two brothers could be so different, and if Colin had resembled either of them.

When Mark was so nice to her she found it bewildering that her thoughts should cling so consistently to Paul. Even her glance was inclined to desert him in favour of Paul. Always Paul's stronger personality dominated, yet intuition warned her that she would be wiser to concentrate on someone else.

This evening Paul was striking in a dark dinner jacket and pants, superbly tailored to his tall, elegant figure. Last night he had been wearing a lounge suit, and she wondered if he was going out.

'I am later,' he said, when she asked.

He sat idly on the sofa beside her and she immediately felt cold. All day she had looked forward eagerly to spending the evening with him, and he was going out!

'I wish you weren't,' she whispered despondently.

Mark had gone to get himself another drink. Mary and John were still upstairs. There was nothing to divert her attention from Paul, who must easily have been able to read the disappointment racing through her.

'Why don't you want me to go out?' he asked softly. 'I have a date.'

Jane frowned fretfully, reluctant to think of him with another woman. 'I haven't seen you since this morning.'

'Are you deliberately reminding me of that?'

'No!' How could he be so nasty? I meant I haven't seen you all day!'

'You have enough company.'

She couldn't deny it. Unless she was in her room she was rarely alone for a moment. 'Your parents and the servants couldn't be kinder,' she allowed with bent head, 'but I'd rather have you.'

'Because you saw too much of me in hospital,' Paul retorted curtly. 'A situation like this has its dangers, Jane. I've told you I don't intend stepping into Colin's shoes, and you'd better believe it.'

When she lifted her face to him again there was bewilderment in her eyes. She couldn't agree that she was thinking of him as a second husband, but she would be lost without him. That he was frequently impatient with her didn't make him any less essential.

'I don't want to find a substitute for C-Colin,' she stammered awkwardly.

'Don't you—I wonder?'

'You're always doubting me, aren't you?' Her blue eyes widened indignantly.

'Right now I'm doubting your age,' he snapped shortly. 'I'm wondering how you can look and act sixteen when you're supposed to be ten years older.'

'You think I'm a child?'

'Not altogether.' His eyes said mockingly to the shadowed cleft between her breasts before swerving to their enticing fulness. 'I realise you're quite grown up and can understand why men find you attractive. If you're childish it's only because you believe you can have everything you want, and it just isn't possible.'

Jane wondered how she would have replied if his parents hadn't arrived, but she didn't get another chance to speak to him alone. After dinner he went out, ignoring her entreating glance, and later, in bed, she was so exhausted she fell asleep without the aid of even one sleeping pill and and had no idea what time he came home.

A week later, John Denyer bought her a beautiful new car, an extremely smart sports model. Jane fell in love with it straight away, although she also viewed it with some dismay. She wasn't sure that she could afford to run a car, or even drive it. On top of this, she tried not to imagine Paul's acid comments when he learnt of his parents giving her such an expensive present.

Mary, sensing she was about to protest, drew her aside as her husband supervised its arrival and begged her quietly not to.

'I realise it's not easy for you, dear. You're so very independent, it's difficult to get you to take anything, but John has been so pleased over this. He adored Colin, you see, and he's so grateful to have you here. Planning small things to give you seems to help him a lot.'

If only he would stick to small things! Yet John's generosity, as well as Mary's, made Jane feel extremely humble. 'I don't know what I've done to deserve you,' she confessed, overwhelmed.

'John and I often wonder the same thing about you,' Mary smiled gently. 'Colin couldn't have chosen a girl we liked better for his wife. We consider ourselves very lucky.'

Paul, surprisingly said very little, other than insisting she didn't attempt to drive the new car until her memory returned and she discovered if she had a licence.

'If we'd known what your name was before you were married it would have been easy to check,' he said coldly, 'but if you hadn't been wearing Colin's signet ring we might not even have known you were his wife.'

Jane tried to argue with him as little as possible these days. Her relationship with him was becoming the most important thing in her life. She continually sought him out when he was at home, although he wasn't always pleasant to her. At the best of times he was less than encouraging, frequently saying hurtful things, making Jane furious with herself that she couldn't accept that he appeared to have no wish to have much to do with her.

When she had been at Coombe Park about three weeks, Paul went abroad for a few days. She wasn't aware he had gone until his mother told her.

'He didn't mention it,' Jane said, unaware of how despondent she sounded.

Mary glanced at her thoughtfully. 'It was a bit of a rush, I believe. Something came up after lunch, apparently, but he did spare the time to give me a ring. I expect he thought I would tell you.'

'Yes.' Jane tried to hide the sudden sense of loss which consumed her. 'Don't you mind?'

'Of course not,' Mary smiled. 'Paul's not usually at home anyway, it's not often I know what he's doing. And I'm used to the ways of international business. After all, John hasn't been retired long.'

'Where has Paul gone?' Jane asked carefully.

'Italy.'

'Oh.' Jane's face paled. 'Isn't that where Colin and I were?'

'It's just one of the countries Paul visits,' Mary said quickly. 'I hope you're not upset. Perhaps I shouldn't have said anything.'

'It doesn't matter,' Jane forced herself to speak lightly, 'I don't suppose Paul's journey has anything to do with me.'

The following days seemed very long and dreary. To try and counteract this, Jane spent a lot of time taking

the dogs for walks in the wooded grounds and helping
Mary with the gardening. A contract firm took care of
most of the big jobs, but Mary still did a lot of the
planting and weeding. Jane was a good worker and it
gave her some satisfaction to believe she was doing
something towards earning her keep.

While she loved being out of doors, assisting Mary
and basking in her approval, it was discovering she
could type which pleased her most. She knew there was
a typewriter in the study, which was also the library,
but she hadn't taken much notice of it until one wet
afternoon when she went to find a book. A lot of
machinery was still an enigma to her. She had found it
frustrating, when she had first come from hospital, that
she didn't know how to use a simple hair-dryer, a piece
of equipment she must have been familiar with all her
life.

The cover was off the typewriter, whereas it was
usually on. This was perhaps what drew Jane's
attention to it. There was even a piece of paper inserted,
as if someone had been going to write something but
had been called away. Idly Jane let her fingers span the
keys while she gazed at it curiously. She hit one or two
of them tentatively, then, to her astonishment, her
fingers were suddenly flying.

'I must have been able to do this before,' she exclaimed to Mark excitedly when, later in the day he came
searching for her. After receiving Mary's amused permission, she had found more paper and a book, which
she was copying from. 'Would you say so?' She showed
him what she had done, seeking his opinion eagerly.

'It certainly looks like it.' He examined the sheets she
handed him carefully. 'This is extremely well done,
quite professional. You appear to have been well
trained.' He glanced from Jane to the typewriter and
back again cautiously. 'Has discovering you can type
brought anything else back?'

'Nothing,' she had been hoping it would and didn't

attempt to conceal her own disappointment, 'but I'm sure I must have worked in an office.'

'It's possible,' he admitted.

'Yet if I worked in an office,' Jane frowned, 'what was I doing in Italy? According to Paul, I wasn't there on holiday.'

'I shouldn't guess, if I were you, Jane,' Mark advised anxiously. 'You've found a machine, not your memory, I'm afraid, and you could do more harm than good, trying to force it.'

Nevertheless, despite Mark's advice, Jane thought a lot about being able to type, and gradually she began seeing pictures of a desk and a hazy room. Unfortunately this was all, but it seemed a start. It bothered her that whenever she tried to concentrate on remembering anything clearly, her heart would begin to race, making her feel faint and generally shaken.

'I told you to be patient,' Mark sighed, finding her like a ghost one day and guessing the reason. 'Go on like this and my head will roll when Paul comes home. I had orders to look after you.'

'Why didn't you tell me this before?' she rounded on him fiercely until she saw how astonished he looked.

'Don't worry,' he smiled, 'Paul didn't ask me to act as a jailor. He just said I was to make sure you didn't do too much—which,' he added dryly, 'seems to be exactly what you're doing!'

'I'm sorry,' Jane faltered, party relieved that Mark had obviously mistaken her reaction for panic. She had believed his brother had left without giving her a thought, and while Mark's confession might not have revealed any great concern on Paul's behalf, it did seem to prove she hadn't been entirely forgotten.

CHAPTER THREE

PAUL returned at the end of a beautiful week in late summer. Jane, just about to enter the house from the gardens, where she had been playing with the dogs, heard the car and ran back to meet him.

He was driving himself, and as he slammed the car door she clutched his arm, the eyes she raised to his face glowing with surprised delight.

'It's lovely to have you home again!' she cried, the excitement inside her sweeping her forward to kiss his cheek. He looked brown, his hard, lean body superbly fit. 'When did you get in?' she asked breathlessly.

'This morning.'

'Oh, I see.' He was rubbing his cheek coolly where she had kissed him, making her feel embarrassed. Aware of colour creeping to her face, she said quickly, 'You must have been to your office.'

'No,' he studied her intently, his voice grim, 'I had other business to attend to.'

'Well, it's good to have you back.' She decided not to ask any more questions which he clearly had no intention of answering.

'Missed me?' To her surprise he suddenly slipped an arm round her waist. Bending his mouth to hers, he returned her kiss with a pressure that startled her.

As he let go of her, as abruptly as he had hauled her to him, she thought she caught a glimpse of harsh aversion in his eyes. And while she was trying to convince herself she had imagined it, he said coldly, 'Hello, Colin's wife.'

Feeling sick, Jane jerked away, her eyes wide and wary. 'Why did you say that?' she whispered, trembling.

41

Instantly he apologised. 'I'm sorry if I hurt you. Perhaps I was reminding myself.'

Jane clenched lips still stinging from the assault of his. Didn't that sound a bit too smooth? Why did she have the feeling that he was goading her deliberately, with something specific on his mind?

'Let's go in,' he suggested, taking scant notice of her obvious uneasiness. With his hand still on her waist, he turned her towards the house. 'How have things been?'

She wasn't sure if he was asking how things had been with her, personally, but she suddenly had no wish to talk about herself. There wasn't much to talk about anyway, and all at once she was too apprehensive of Paul's mockery to confess she had been counting the hours till his return.

'Your parents are visiting some old friends,' she remembered their names and when she told him he nodded. 'I believe,' she said, 'they're staying for dinner.'

'And Mark's dining in town.'

Her heart sank. Paul was unlikely to want to stay here with her alone. 'Will you be joining him?' she asked.

'Not a chance!' he grinned wickedly. 'Mark has a date with a fabulous blonde. I wouldn't dare suggest it.'

'You must know plenty yourself.'

'I'm not exactly short of similar acquaintances,' he agreed sardonically, 'but this evening I feel more interested in someone with—different coloured hair. Isn't there a song about a girl with light brown hair?'

'She's Jeannie, not Jane.'

'Well, nearly.'

They reached the lounge, after Paul had been welcomed by James, who had instructed a maid to bring tea. While they drank it Paul had little to say. Jane couldn't accuse him of being neglectful, but occasionally she caught him giving her what looked like a hard-eyed stare. She told herself she was being over-sensitive. If he did sometimes look grim, it might have nothing to do with her. His thoughts were probably on business matters, miles away!

'Won't you tell me about your trip?' she forced herself to ask, knowing she was reluctant to mention it. 'You were in Italy, I believe?'

'Yes,' he replied curtly, 'I had a conference to attend, after which I took a couple of days off to—enjoy the sunshine.'

Who with? she wondered, aware of his slight hesitation, her heart suddenly heavy.

'The weather must have been fine.' She pretended to admire his tan, making it an excuse for allowing her eyes to linger on his face. 'You're certainly brown!'

Paul laughed, his eyes crinkling. 'Come upstairs and I'll fill in all the details, if you like.' Putting down his cup, he jumped lithely to his feet. 'Come on, I'm longing for a shower. I'm even tempted to try the pool.'

As they walked hand in hand upstairs, and she waited for him to decide, his gaze slanted to her thoughtfully. 'Have you tried the pool yet?' he asked.

Arriving at his room, as he pulled her gently inside, she shook her head. 'I don't know if I can swim.'

'Shall we find out?'

'I'm going to—one day.'

'No time like the present.'

'But I haven't a costume, Paul.' Jane wasn't sure that she was keen on the idea. Mark had tried to persuade her to visit the pool, so had Mary, but when she'd held back they hadn't insisted. Paul did, though. Unlike the other members of his family he didn't allow her all her own way.

'There's bound to be something lying around you can wear. If not, you can go in without. I won't look.'

She couldn't believe he intentionally meant to shake her, that this was all part of a diabolically planned campaign. She watched, oddly breathless, as he searched through some drawers, then found a pair of black trunks.

'I knew they must be here somewhere!' he said triumphantly. 'Come on!'

His ruthless grip on her arm seemed to leave her no choice. In the covered pool which lay at the end of the summer-house, she found a costume of sorts. It was old and shrunken, the colour faded.

Paul laughed when he saw her in it. 'That belonged to my mother,' he told her.

'Does she swim?'

'She used to.'

Jane sat on the edge of the pool, wishing he would stop looking at her. The costume stretched uncomfortably, for all she was slender and not very tall. She gazed at the water, dipping her toes in reluctantly.

'Aren't we brave!' he jeered, diving sardonically, in a clear-cut arch, disappearing under the water, causing scarcely a ripple. Surfacing immediately, he swam back to her, his eyes glinting. 'Come on, you little coward!'

'Maybe I can't swim?'

'Of course you can!'

She wondered why he was so sure, but at that moment she was concentrating on the pool more than on what he was saying. She decided against going in. Paul might taunt her, but what were words? He would be too frightened of hurting her to use force. Leaning over to tell him she was staying where she was, he startled her by reaching out and pulling her on top of him.

At least, she might have been on top of him if he hadn't twisted away. With a cry of alarm she hit the water, swallowing mouthfuls as she sank like a stone. She hadn't time to be angry, she was too busy trying to save herself from drowning.

Then, to her amazement, just as she had discovered she could type, she found she could swim. Her first helpless flounderings soon changed to more practised movements, rapidly dissolving her fears. Twice she swam round the pool, feeling pleased with herself, almost ready to forgive Paul for pulling her in.

When at last she climbed out, he was waiting for her. Triumphantly she smiled at him. 'I can swim!'

'Yes.' His voice was suddenly harsh.

He had been watching her performance, but he sounded as if he had known beforehand. Yet how could he? As he returned with a sharp plunge to the water, Jane followed his progress with bewilderment in her eyes. Perhaps she was getting too fanciful? It must be foolish to imagine Paul had intended sitting down beside her until a sudden surge of anger had caused him to change his mind.

He had probably guessed she could swim because most young people were taught at school and there was no reason to suppose she had been any different from the rest. Her own unconscious fears might be easily explained. She hadn't told him, there hadn't been time, how she had woken that morning from a vivid dream. It hadn't been a nightmare, exactly, though she had found it rather alarming. She had been wandering in a place she didn't recognise, other than that it was warm and not English. The dream had remained with her all day, developing and gaining depth when most dreams usually fade. She had seen a stranger with a camera coming from a hotel. There had been another girl with the man with the camera and, together, they had chased Jane into the sea.

Realising Paul was coming back to her, Jane couldn't decide what to do. She might mention discovering she was able to type and forget about the dream. At this stage it was unlikely to throw any great light on her past, and, despite the short break he'd said he had taken, Paul looked tired.

When he heaved himself from the water at last, he appeared to have regained his humour. Jane had wrapped herself in a towel, but he didn't bother. As her eyes clung to his powerful body, she wished he would.

With water streaming off him, making his skin glisten, he was undeniably attractive, with enough virility to make her heart race.

Superbly masculine! She seemed to have heard those words before, not long ago. Despondently she sighed, then gave up, concentrating unconsciously on Paul. His chest was covered with curling wet hairs, as dark as his head. Without thinking, as she had done when he had stayed with her all night, she allowed her hand to creep forward until her fingertips touched him.

'You need my dryer,' she said.

She saw his jaw set. 'Lady, you're playing with fire.'

Was that a joke connecting with her remark? Frustration flicked her as she wished she wasn't always so slow to catch on. 'How?' she queried.

'My God!' he grasped hold of her suddenly, bringing her palm flat against his chest, 'I've been idling in a warm climate for days without a woman and you have to ask that!'

Now he really shocked her, and, ignoring her incredulous gasp, he went on doing it. Taking her other hand, before she could escape, he held it against him also.

'You don't have to feel deprived in any way,' he taunted. 'Help yourself.'

His ruthless features swam before her eyes as a suffusion of warmth swept through her. For a moment she struggled until curiosity and sensation won. 'I've never been close to anyone like this before,' she muttered dazedly.

'Disregarding having slept in my arms?'

'A—apart from that.'

'How do you know?

Her eyes dilated with trying to think, she blinked. 'I suppose you're right—I don't.'

'Never mind,' he laughed though his eyes darkened, 'why bother discussing the past? A part of your memory might be missing, but you seem to have more than your fair share of everything else!'

Before she could move, he caught her to him. Letting go of her hands, he slid his round her back, expertly throwing her towel aside at the same time. Then he lowered his head and his mouth came down on hers hard.

A great panic surged over Jane, as overwhelming as the water she had just left. She thought her already racing heart was about to jump out of her body. Paul's strong lips exerted pressure, as if he felt her fright and was determined to subdue it. His arms tightened, pinning her to him, engulfing them both in a tide of erotic passion. She grew breathless from the suffocating heat and hardness of his mouth, the exquisite torture of her own emotions. But it wasn't until the feelings within her grew uncontrollable, exploding in panic, that she found the strength to push him away.

'I wish you wouldn't do that!' she gasped.

She heard his breath suck in as his chest heaved, yet his voice when he spoke was cool with amusement. 'I've only kissed you once before. Surely your memory is that functional?'

'I'm sorry.' She was unable to understand herself in any way that made sense. She wanted to be near Paul, but this close she panicked. 'I feel peculiar,' she protested weakly.

'So do I,' he replied dryly.

She wished he would stop staring at her, almost as much as she wished she could move. Their faces were very close, his silvery gaze hypnotising her, grey eyes mocking, his mouth hard and firm. Helplessly she gazed at that mouth as he slowly reached for the straps of her costume, pushing them from her shoulders.

'You're beautiful,' he said thickly, surveying her half naked body, its enticing hollows and curves.

'Please, Paul,' she entreated, 'I'd like to get dressed.'

'I dare say you would, but I'd like to make love to you,' he muttered huskily.

'No!' She didn't want to deny him a thing and her heart was beating wildly, betraying her. She might protest for hours and he wouldn't believe her.

His caressing hands proved it. She could almost feel the determination in them as they moved to the slender swell of her hips, rendering her like candle wax under their persuasive pressure. Her muscles must have melted, for she couldn't feel them.

He rubbed his wet cheek against hers, his lips brushing her skin lightly. "Put your arms round me,' he commanded, an instant before his mouth found hers again and he bent her ruthlessly backwards.

It was the hardness of the tiles underneath her and the crush of his hard body against her breasts that jerked Jane back to reality. In a moment of pain she became suddenly aware of the dangers of the situation. Immediately, despite the flames threatening to consume her, she began fighting the traitorous inclinations of her arms and mind. Fiercely she beat at Paul with clenched fists, twisting from the sensuous heaviness of his hardening limbs and urgent mouth.

Eventually, with a grunt of disgust, he let her go. Springing to his feet, he grated, 'I've never had to fight for my fun yet, and I don't intend to start!'

Jane gasped, brushing tumbled hair and distracted tears from her face. He had spoken to her with less respect than he would a tramp! Horrified, she recoiled, wondering what he was trying to do to her. Had he been secretly disapproving that she had agreed to come here with him? Disapproving and determined to teach her a lesson?

'I should have stayed at the house,' she whispered, eyes huge in a white face.

He yanked her up beside him as she straightened her untidy costume. 'Perhaps you should,' he agreed half impatiently, 'but, in persuading you not to, I was as much to blame.'

Such magnanimity, after such anger, confused her. It seemed too good to be true. If it were true . . .?

'Stop looking at me so suspiciously,' he grinned. 'Why not exchange olive branches and go out for dinner? Somewhere not too quiet, where I won't be tempted to break the good resolutions I'm busy making!'

Jane found it difficult to believe how, ten minutes later, they could be walking back to the house, both decorously dressed, acting as though nothing had happened. She still felt shaken and uneasy, but did her best to hide it. If Paul could be generous, wasn't it up to her to meet him halfway? If she sulked he might only think less of her, and she couldn't bear it when he looked at her with censure in his eyes.

In her room she touched her lips with trembling fingers. She could feel his kisses there in every nerve of her body. Flushing painfully, she recalled telling him that she was sure she had never been as close to a man before, and how this mouth had twisted cynically. As she had been married, he must think she was crazy! Would she never learn? she wondered unhappily, going to the bathroom to begin washing her sticky hair.

Feeling oddly exhausted, she would rather have stayed at home for dinner, but she hadn't liked to argue with Paul when he had insisted they went out. He had promised he would avoid the more intimate places, but the nightclub he took her to seemed to go to the other extreme. It was very noisy. He must be in a strange mood, she decided, gazing doubtfully at the slightly garish surroundings, for she couldn't believe that normally such a place would appeal to him.

As the evening progressed she grew more and more bewildered. Paul scarcely spoke to her throughout the meal they ate, and afterwards he made her dance with him, holding her far too close. When she stumbled against him, he made an unkind remark which hurt her terribly. At one in the morning, when she pleaded to go home, he merely asked insolently if she was bored.

He apologised later, as they left, although neither his apology nor the gist of it seemed to ring true. 'I get very restless after being abroad. You'll have to forgive me.'

Jane nodded, shrugging off a fleeting suspicion that no amount of overseas travel would affect him that much. She was sure he had, for some reason, been acting out of character, but when he smiled at her she found herself smiling weakly back, forgiving him. When Paul Denyer turned on the charm she believed few women would be able to resist him.

When they got home though her anxiety returned as she realised everyone was in bed. 'I shouldn't have gone out,' she worried. 'I hope your parents won't think . . .'

'That you've forgotten Colin?' Paul suggested dryly, as she hesitated. 'They must know it's bound to happen some time.'

That might be true, but she hated the way he put it. 'Normally,' she retorted, 'a girl wouldn't forget her husband so soon.'

'If they heard you come in and say anything—which I think unlikely—tell them I was enjoying myself and refused to leave the club.'

Jane sighed. 'Your parents aren't that easily fooled.'

'Jane,' Paul snapped impatiently, 'go to bed! Do you imagine I'm a schoolboy, having to account for my every movement? I'm only living here just now as my mother is concerned for you. I hope to God she isn't in for a rude awakening!'

Jane stared at him. He seemed to imply that it was bound to happen. 'Concerning you?'

'No, you!'

She frowned, her eyes hollow orbs of bewilderment in an exhausted face. 'I care for your mother a lot . . .'

'I'm sure,' he broke in grimly. 'Jane,' he reiterated forcibly, 'I don't want to hear any more. If you're not out of my sight in two seconds, I might shake you!'

Jane fled, trembling at his barely leashed intolerance. She failed to understand, when he did his best to bend her to his will, why he should despise her for giving in to him. In future, she would have as little to do with him as possible. She would concentrate on trying to remember her recent marriage and not give Paul another opportunity of accusing her of forgetting!

She was tired the next morning and overslept. It was after eleven when she found Mary in the garden and apologised to her. 'I seem to be getting terribly lazy,' she said.

The dogs came rushing to meet her, expecting her to play with them, their tails wagging.

'Hello, you darlings!' She bent over them, the sunlight glinting on her silky brown hair. It was growing long enough to have to be brushed out of her eyes and she hoped the fuss the dogs were making would divert Mary's attention from her rather lame excuse. 'They're full of beans today, aren't they?' she laughed, emerging at last from a surfeit of persuasive whimpers and lolling tongues. 'I kept an eye on them for you yesterday, but I think they missed you.'

'They don't appear to have suffered from it.' Mary patted Thor, the big labrador, idly. Shrewdly her eyes rested on Jane's flushed face. 'Paul told me he kept you out late.'

Jane gulped, feeling terribly guilty. 'You've seen him?'

Mary smiled. 'We had breakfast together.'

How much had Paul told her? Biting her lip, her eyes anxious, Jane wished she knew. 'Perhaps I shouldn't have gone out with him—or anyone, not so—so soon. I hope you don't mind?'

'No, Jane, and I don't disapprove, if that's what you mean.' Mary laid a gentle hand on her arm. 'I shouldn't like you to be hurt, though.' As Jane continued looking at her uncertainly, she hesitated. 'I'm not quite sure how to put this, dear, but you've been hurt once and I shouldn't want it to happen again, if in a different way. Paul means to be kind, he thought an outing would do you good, but I feel he might be kinder to leave you alone.'

Mary's words held enough wisdom to keep Jane pondering for hours. When Paul didn't return that evening she decided Mary must have spoken to him as well, yet far from resenting what some might have viewed as interference, she felt grateful. If she was to avoid Paul in future, she recognised she might need help.

The following morning, however, when he rang and invited her to go to a concert with him that evening, Jane realised that though his mother might have warned him tactfully to keep his distance, he wasn't apparently going to take her advice.

'I'm not sure.' Jane hated the way she faltered when all she had to do was refuse, but desire was building up inside her so feverishly, she couldn't bring herself to utter a definite no.

'I'm too busy to argue,' he said shortly. 'I'll pick you up at seven. We'll eat first.'

So much for her good resolutions, Jane thought wearily, as he rang off. She must have about as much willpower as a mouse! She didn't know what she was going to tell her mother-in-law, but in the end fate seemed to solve the problem for her when Mary's brother rang from the West Country, inviting her and John to pay him a short visit.

In the ensuing flurry of activity, Jane tried to pretend there wasn't time to mention Paul's invitation. In any case, she would have hesitated to worry Mary, as the thought of seeing her brother, and perhaps getting away for a few days, put the first real animation Jane had seen into Mary's eyes.

'You should be coming with us,' said Mary, as she and John departed. 'Richard lives on his own and is getting very frail, but he does have a good housekeeper. I'm sure he would be pleased to see you.'

'Perhaps the next time,' Jane smiled, waving them goodbye. The change would do them both good—but her face sobered wistfully as their car disappeared down the drive. Although they would only be away two nights, she would miss them.

Paul, elegant in dark evening clothes, collected her at the stroke of seven. Jane, having taken extra care over her own appearance, thought they must make a well matched couple. Flushing, that such a thought should cross her mind, she hastened to tell him about his parents.

'They were in touch,' he said, so laconically she felt like hitting him. 'Do you think they would have dreamt of leaving their little ewe lamb without first making sure she was going to be looked after?'

'Why does no one ever tell me anything!' Jane retorted indignantly.

'I'm willing to tell you how charming you look in that black thing you're wearing,' he drawled, as they drove back to London. 'Not that's there's much visible under the fur jacket, but my imagination's having a field day!'

'I thought it might be cold later,' she explained.

'I could keep you warm.'

His voice was so cool, it must be his words which scorched her. She suspected it was a deliberate gibe and didn't reply.

His glance slanted over her shining head, her delicately made up face, to rest again on the jacket. 'First a car, now furs, at a guess costing not much less. Where did you get it?'

'Your mother.' She clutched the jacket with nervous fingers, as his glance suggested he would like to rape her of it. 'She—she said it hadn't cost much.'

'And you believed her?'

'Why shouldn't I?'

'Oh, lady!' he drawled, with a soft menace. 'You're certainly asking for everything that's coming to you!'

'Paul,' she straightened away from him, terror showing unconsciously on her small face, "I had no particular wish to go out with you this evening.'

'Liar!'

'You can turn round and take me straight home.'

He drove straight on, whistling softly for a moment under his breath. 'You don't really want me to, do you?'

Unhappily she glanced out of the car window. Because he had called her a liar it made her determined to stick to the truth, but he didn't make it easy for her. 'No,' she admitted reluctantly, 'but I'd rather spend the evening alone if you're going to be horrible to me all the time.'

'I'm sorry,' he murmured, already parking at the end of a street, which didn't give her much chance to discover if that meant he meant to reform.

The restaurant where Paul had a table booked was a complete contrast to the one he had taken her to two evenings before. It wasn't small, but it was quiet and exclusive and their arrival attracted a great deal of discreet attention. It must be Paul, Jane decided. He was striking enough to attract attention anywhere. For herself, she disliked being stared at, and she was aware of Paul's faint amusement as his silvery glance caught the warmth of selfconscious colour in her cheeks.

'Have I a smut on my nose or something, or is it you?' she asked, softly indignant as they sat down.

Paul smiled, a complacent, tigerish twist of his lips. 'We make a good-looking couple, don't you think?'

This was such an echo of her previous thoughts that the colour in her cheeks immediately deepened. 'Such a thought never crossed my mind,' she denied primly, recalling too late how she had vowed never to lie to him, only a few minutes ago. Simply being evasive didn't come into that category, surely?

'What does cross your mind, I wonder?' Paul

drawled, apparently making idle conversation. 'I'd give a lot to find out.'

'Nothing much,' she hedged, hoping he never guessed he was on it almost continually.

'That I can't believe,' he retorted with an oddness of manner which made her shiver, though she imagined he meant to be complimentary.

Uncertainly she smiled at him, relieved to find nothing in his expressionless face to justify her fleeting uneasiness. The waiter arrived with the menu and by the time they had discussed it and ordered, Paul was being so nice to her that she was only aware of a glow of happiness.

The feeling lasted throughout the meal and the concert which followed, given by the London Symphony Orchestra. Jane found the music both soothing and stimulating. Not being able to remember yet what kind of music she had enjoyed before her accident, she was startled by the depth of her own response, but when Paul held her hand occasionally, causing positive flickers of flame to rush through her, she began thinking she must be a very emotional person.

When the concert was over, he insisted on visiting his apartment for coffee. She presumed it was a service flat when he said, 'I had some sandwiches sent up earlier. It seems a pity to waste them.'

She went with him reluctantly, trying to disguise a tremor of panic as she followed him into a luxurious set of rooms. It was part of a huge block, complete with uniformed commissionaire and obviously every electronic device to ensure the safety and privacy of its occupants. There was quietness here, a relaxed atmosphere, so why did every nerve in her body feel tense?

'I'm really not hungry,' she said awkwardly, as Paul relieved her of her coat. She wasn't willing to part with it as it seemed to indicate he was contemplating a long stay.

'Coffee?'

Feeling she might be gaining ground, she shook her head.

'A drink, then?'

Knowing she couldn't refuse again without arousing his suspicions, she allowed him to pour her one. She tried not to watch his tall, lean figure, the black hair faintly flecked with silver at his temples, the same silver she sometimes saw in his eyes.

She leaned back against the sofa, breathing quickly, finding it difficult to control her irrational fears. Paul was such an enigma, she never could decide whether he was being kind to her or cruel. She watched him select a bottle and two glasses from a cabinet against the wall. Without asking what she liked, he poured a generous measure of spirits into each, splashing soda liberally into hers.

'You look as if you need a drink,' he commented dryly, making her realise he was clearly aware of the apprehension she was doing her best to hide. Without attempting to move he said softly, 'Are you coming to get it, or shall I join you?'

Her glance darted over the sofa; it was too deep and long, she would feel too much at his mercy. Without attempting to define such feelings, she moved swiftly to join him, an unconscious fluidity of limbs giving her a grace which narrowed the grey eyes watching her approach.

'You move beautifully,' he said thoughtfully, his eyes trained fully on her. 'No wonder you attract men.'

Jane took the glass he gave her, swallowing the whisky with a grimace. She drank it off like medicine, hoping for immediate results, but rather than steady her pulse it only made it race faster.

The warmth of the spirit, however, running through her veins, did give her enough courage to shrug lightly. Whatever happened, she wasn't going to enter into another argument with him about that. He liked taunting her, but he had no real evidence that men found her attractive.

Her indifference appeared to annoy him, because his eyes glinted icily as he tipped up his glass. As he turned to refill it, she despised herself for allowing her glance to feast on his broad shoulders, the arrogant set of his dark head.

'Do you think that's wise?' she queried. 'You know,' as he turned and his brows rose, 'drinking and driving?'

'Oh, I'll give it time to get out of my bloodstream,' he assured her carelessly.

A stab of dismay prompted Jane to exclaim, 'We ought to be getting back!'

'Your party line,' he observed gently.

Distrusting the softness of his voice, she tried again. 'I promised your mother . . .'

'She's always forgetting how children grow up,' he smiled. 'I have to remind her. In your case she believes she's dealing with an entirely different kind of girl, and until you move on, you'll just have to put up with her, I'm afraid.'

What was Paul saying, or trying to say? While she was searching for the answer, Jane allowed her glance to wander around the room. It was a huge room, with wide windows. She imagined the view would be panoramic, even at night, although this evening the curtains were drawn, as if against any intrusion, even of moonlight. The colours were restful, fawns, golds and soft browns with lots of creamy white. It was a room clearly designed for relaxation and she was curious about the friends Paul invited here. Most of them were probably women.

Helplessly, faintly chilled, her glance returned to him. The mocking glint in his eyes betrayed him amused by her dilemma. 'I do intend moving on,' she said anxiously, 'as soon as my memory returns and I find someone willing to take me in.'

'Don't you mean,' he asked softly, 'that as soon as

you find a man willing to take you in, your memory might return?'

Her eyes widened incredulously as his mouth snapped shut. 'I'm talking of finding a room, not a man! I keep feeling . . .' she paused, shrugging distractedly, 'It's only a hazy impression, but I feel I've shared with someone, lived with someone. I'm not talking about Colin.'

'I'm sure you're right,' Paul said silkily, his eyes hard as diamonds.

Jane was hopelessly caught in their glittering depth. As usual he was too clever for her, always one step— no, miles ahead, and she never seemed able to catch up. She was sure she had shared a flat of some kind with other girls, and it suddenly was important to convince him. Yet how could she when she had no proof, no clear recollections?

'Let me refill your glass,' she heard him offer, as if they had been merely discussing the weather.

'Paul! I'm serious,' she pleaded unhappily. 'We ought to go home. It's not sensible to stay here.'

Removing the glass from her nerveless fingers, he smiled gently, staring straight in her eyes. 'Would you care to be more explicit?'

She flushed, swallowing convulsively. He was asking her to explain feelings which she didn't really understand herself. 'What will people think?' she murmured evasively.

His harsh bark of laughter made her shrink. 'That's the last thing I should have thought a girl like you would be worried about!'

She went white. 'A girl like me?'

He swore under his breath and she tensed, fearing he was going to hit her. She drew a sharp breath, but he didn't move. Then after a taut pause, he said curtly, 'I don't intend to be insulting, Jane, but you can't pretend you haven't been around.'

CHAPTER FOUR

JANE stared at him, wishing she could deny it, her blue eyes dark with frustration. If she had been living in Italy when she met his brother, it seemed more than likely that Paul was talking sense.

'I wish I could remember!' she whispered shakily, the palms of her hands damp with sweat.

She heard a sharp noise as he disposed of their glasses, then gasped as his fingers firmly lifted her chin. 'Perhaps I can help you?' he drawled, drawing her slowly into his arms.

She wasn't sure of his intentions, but even trying to guess filled her with alarm. 'No, Paul!'

'Lady,' he laughed, 'I'm sure that's new word in your vocabulary!'

'Oh, please!' She tried to twist from his grip, suddenly terrified by his insistence. Intuition told her she would be crazy to let him help her in any way at all, that his gentle smiles and soft words cloaked a malignity against which she might never survive.

'Be quiet!' he said roughly.

Jane closed her eyes to shut out the disturbing darkness of his face. To her shame, as his lips moved over her cheek she was filled with an immediate sense of anticipation. A mad trembling took hold of her as he seemed to be bending her to his strength and will. Her slightest movement brought her into closer contact with his hard, muscled body, forcing her to stand completely still.

'It may please you to act the little innocent with your big blue eyes,' he muttered coolly, 'but I know what you want. What the whole of you is crying out for.'

'How can you?' she cried, her voice muffled against

his chest but clearly bewildered. 'I don't even know myself!'

He lifted a hand, trailing it lightly across her breast. 'Doesn't that tell you anything?'

'No!' Paul shocked her to the very depth of her being when he touched her like that. It was a complete contradiction of the revulsion she felt that she should want him to touch her again. The terrible clamouring of desire she experienced couldn't be real. 'If you don't let me go,' she gulped, 'I'll scream!'

As if her wild threats angered him, his hard hands bit into her skin. Her alarmed glance saw that the grey eyes were no longer even scornfully tolerant. Only too clearly she recognised the determination blazing in them and she was horrified to find her body trembling in response.

Paul watched her intently, his eyes smouldering, then slowly his mouth took possession of hers. His hands seemed to be everywhere and, as her lips parted, they drew her closer, moving down her body to press her in towards him. Involuntarily she clutched at him, as the strength left her legs, and an electric shock flashed through her as her fingers came in contact with the warmth of his chest. She could feel the heat of his flesh though the thin silk of his shirt communicating with her burning palms sliding against him. Beads of perspiration broke out all over her. Frantically she tried to ease away, but the grip of his hands was unbreakable on her hips.

She felt fright building up until she was sure she might faint, yet as soon as he stopped kissing her, her mouth opened in silent protest, wanting to be possessed again. The glitter in his eyes might have brought her to her senses if she hadn't been lost to everything but the burning demands of her own body.

'Paul,' she whispered, totally at the mercy of the throbbing, pulsating sweetness inside her, unable to understand what was happening to her.

As she gasped his name, his low laughter was harsh as he bent his lips to her throat. 'Tired of fighting, sweetheart?'

The derision in his voice made a mockery of the endearment. She stiffened, but he didn't allow any resistance. When she began struggling to get away from him, he picked her up like a feather, dropping her into the depth of the couch. She had a hazy impression of his jacket flying to a chair before he came down beside her, depleting her further of her already shortened breath.

'Much better than standing around, don't you think?' he muttered sarcastically, gathering her to him as he slipped the narrow straps from her shoulders so her dress fell almost to her waist.

The expertise and swiftness of his movements stunned Jane. Her face went quite white, her limbs paralysed with shock. She remembered thinking, by the pool at Coombe Park, that he made her feel like a tramp. Now the same thought occurred.

She sat up, protesting huskily, 'Paul, I want to go home!'

Wordlessly he pushed her back against the cushions, raising himself on an elbow to study her. Dazed, she watched his eyes narrow as he looked for the fastening on her bra, saw them glitter with cynical amusement as he found it. As he dealt with it, exposing the full contours of her breasts to his smouldering gaze, she nearly died of shame.

She ran a frantic tongue-tip over dry lips. 'Please, don't!'

He ignored her strangled plea. She could feel the insistent probing of his silvery eyes scorching her bare skin, but she was suddenly past caring. She didn't seem able to continue struggling, all her energy was going to fighting her own increasing desire. Her heart was beating so wildly she feared he must feel it as he lowered his mouth to the almost visible movement of it.

She thought she might go mad under his lightly caressing hands which soothed and kneaded beside the increasing pressure of his mouth. Once more she tried to escape, but again his ruthless force pushed her back, his heavy body lowering on her making no secret of his arousal. She was conscious of his hardness hurting her slender limbs while the ache in the lower part of her stomach begged her surrender.

As he heard her soft moan, his mouth returned to hers, biting its way past the throbbing pulse in her throat, hard with sensuous reassurance. 'I won't disappoint you, sweetheart,' he muttered thickly, as her arms went helplessly round his neck.

He had ripped open the buttons of his shirt, now he grazed the fullness of her tender breasts with his hair-roughened skin. He must have been aware of her smothered gasp of pain but he took no notice. Instead he crushed her closer, waiting with the patience of an experienced predator until the urgency of her own desire made her forget any feelings of discomfort.

'Paul!' she gasped, her pleading now for a release of an entirely different kind.

'Tell me you want me!' he commanded hoarsely, his fingers nipping her distended nipples.

Driven mindless, Jane moaned her assent.

His mouth took hers savagely as his hands went to his belt. Vaguely she was conscious of the impatience in them as his control went. Pain and passion mingled as he explored secret areas she was sure no man had ever touched before. Yet, far from being frightened, she found herself responding, her slight body writhing against him, her nails making red marks on his shoulders.

Then suddenly, just when she seemed in danger of being devoured by the heat of his demands, he rolled away from her with a smothered oath.

'Paul?' she murmured, thinking it must be the

hundredth time she had uttered his name. Her head was whirling, she felt bruised and scorched, yet worse than anything was the feeling of being let down. 'Come back,' she whispered, 'please!'

'No,' he replied, so softly, why did she think of the swish of a whip?

Knowing she was abandoned, she broke into wildly hysterical tears, strange tearing sounds coming from her throat as she gasped for breath. When he slapped her face there was a dreadful clamouring in her ears, although the slap was light.

'I'm sorry I had to hit you, Jane,' he said tightly, beginning to straighten his clothes.

Were his hands shaking, or was it just nerves dancing before her eyes? 'Why,' she whispered, staring at him, her face white, 'did you do that?'

He was pale, but his voice was icy. 'I remembered my brother.'

'Colin?' Her eyes were bewildered—he was always remembering Colin. 'But he—he isn't here any more.'

'He can't be forgotten, Jane. Not so soon.'

Hysteria rose again, making her want to shout. 'How can you forget someone you feel you never knew?'

'Jane!' Paul might have guessed her thoughts and been determined not to give her a chance to voice them. 'I think we've both had enough for one night. I'll take you home.'

There seemed nothing more to say, at least nothing she felt she could say that Paul would approve of. Gazing at him with bitter dislike, she allowed him to help her on wth her coat and followed him from the flat.

They scarcely exchanged a word all the way to Coombe Park. Sitting hunched in her seat, Jane kept her eyes closed. She was aware of Paul's dark glance slanting frequently over her, but she felt she would rather die than let him guess how miserable she was. She tried not to think about him, almost as hard as she tried to control the wild spasms of grief which shook her.

When they got in, because she thought he would still be angry, he confused her by smiling at her gently and ordering her straight to bed.

'I'll bring you some hot milk,' he said.

She didn't like to refuse. She was certain, if she did, he would bring it anyway, and she realised, with a hollow feeling of sunken pride, just how far she was willing to unbend to have him smiling at her again.

When he brought it she was in bed, and though his eyes flickered restlessly over her, he merely put it down and said goodnight.

'Paul,' she breathed, as he reached the door.

'Yes?' He didn't turn.

'Are we—still friends?'

'Of course.' This time he did turn. 'If you ever need advice come to me. I'll always be ready to give it.'

Perhaps because she pondered so long on his parting expression and words, the milk grew cold and she had to leave it. Later she regretted not drinking it as she tossed and turned, not falling asleep until dawn. It was afternoon when she woke, feeling terrible. Late hours couldn't agree with her, she reflected wryly, recalling how long she had slept after the first time Paul had taken her out.

Her head was aching badly and she blamed it on what had happened the night before. Paul was right, as her adverse reactions proved; it was too soon to forget Colin. What he didn't seem to understand was that feelings, some kind of feelings, anyway, couldn't be controlled. She was attracted to Paul. Each time he touched her she felt shaken, but that didn't mean she loved him. Whatever love was?

Mrs Finn came clucking up with a tray. Taking one glance at Jane's strained features, she retraced her steps for aspirin. 'I'd stay in bed if I were you, dear,' she advised, her kindly face anxious. 'Mrs John would never forgive me if she thought I was't looking after you properly.'

Jane, managing a smile, said it might do her more good to get some fresh air. 'I don't think I'm used to late nights.'

'Mr Paul ought to know better,' Mrs Finn retorted sharply, 'but you try telling a man of thirty-six that!'

Jane had a shower, but it didn't help. Nevertheless, she made her way to the garden, after swallowing some tea and aspirin. She had been sick in the bathroom, but the aspirin was easing her head. There was a wooded area beyond the main grounds, where she went with the dogs. Sitting under a tree, she tried to relax as she watched them play.

It was cooler today, but she didn't notice as her head still throbbed. Pictures began flashing through it, as if someone was using it as a projector, pushing in slides but flicking them out again before she had time to see them properly. It wasn't until after about an hour that the pictures began getting clearer, taking definite shape and form. Jane suddenly realised she was seeing a kaleidoscope of her life, and immediately her memory returned. Never having imagined it could happen like this, she was filled with a kind of horrified apprehension. One moment her past was a mystery, the next, she could remember everything.

She had never been married to Colin Denyer, she was merely a girl who had flown from Italy with him and his wife. She wouldn't even have known who they were if she hadn't heard the stewardess speaking to them. She didn't suppose she would have learnt their Christian names either, if they hadn't quarrelled loudly all the way. She remembered thinking it amusing that the other girl was called Jane, the same as herself, especially as she had seemed such a shrew!

She shivered, without amusement, as everything came sweeping back. She was Jane Carey, and twenty-one, not twenty-five, and she had never been engaged, let alone

married! With a despairing groan for the muddle she
was in, she buried her face in her hands. An orphan
since ten, the only child of professional parents who
had died without money or relations willing to take their
daughter in, she had been placed in a children's home
which she had left at eighteen. For the next two years
she had worked in a solicitor's office, but the firm had
closed down when the partners had retired.

Having had no luck in finding another office job, she
had reached the stage of being willing to try anything
when a photographer friend of one of the girls she
shared a flat with had suggested she tried modelling.
Thinking she was crazy to be following such advice, she
had gone along to an agency who, to her utter
amazement, agreed she had possibilities.

Jane didn't like recalling the following year, the sheer
hard work, the complete lack of the glamour the
profession was generally imagined to be drenched in.
She received several small jobs and spent any cash she
had left over after keeping herself on training. Italy
had been her first real break and the agency had agreed
to arrange for her to fly home a day earlier than the
others so that she could be bridesmaid at her best
friend's wedding. Her heart sank when she thought of
Beth and the shock she must have received. Whatever
happened, she must get in touch with her as soon as
possible.

At the airport there had been a muddle, but she had
managed to get a flight on one of the smaller airlines.
She had found herself sitting by Colin's wife and soon
realised she wasn't going to enjoy the experience. The
young couple, she soon gathered, hadn't been long
married and were also returning to London in a hurry,
but she was startled when the girl, obviously older than
her husband, began ranting about not wanting to leave,
of having friends and commitments in Italy who were
more important to her than he was.

Jane had hated having to listen and to witness Colin

Denyer's embarrassment and misery. She had done her best not to listen, but the pitch of their voices had been such that every word seemed to reach her unwilling ears. She remembered being convinced that Mrs Denyer was deranged and a bitch! She hated thinking ill of anyone, but could find no other words to describe someone who abused her husband for hours. Jane remembered, too, feeling sorry for the pleasant young man who hadn't seemed able to utter a word in his own defence.

His wife had become even more voluble as they had approached their destination. She began losing control and screaming about a divorce. Colin had tried to quieten her, without success. That was when she had thrust the rings she was wearing at Jane, demanding she should put them on, and because Colin had begged for her help so desperately, Jane had agreed. Reluctantly she pushed them on her finger, believing she might be helping to avert a final, tragic scene, but as soon as she had seen it wasn't going to work she had started to take them off again. She had only been prevented from doing so when the other Jane had flung her handbag at her, just before the crash.

'Oh, God!' Jane gasped aloud, not surprised, when she reached this point, to find she was trembling uncontrollably. The nightmares she had had in hospital had really happened. They hadn't been merely distorted reflections of her imagination. If only her memory had returned sooner, what a lot of trouble it might have saved! When she thought of the sorrow and suffering Colin's parents had already gone through, she couldn't bear to think what this new development was going to do to them. They had lost their son and it had been a terrible blow, but that his wife was still alive had seemed to comfort them greatly. Jane felt a terrifying weight of guilt, as though she had been deceiving them intentionally. She also felt a dreadful sense of loss as she realised how much she had appreciated being part of a proper family again and was going to miss it.

'What am I going to do?' she moaned, not thinking of herself at all but of John and Mary.

She felt utterly confused and really ill. She wasn't sure what she should do. There was just a chance that they might come home today instead of tomorrow. Mary, Jane knew, at the last moment, hadn't been keen to leave her. If they arrived home unexpectedly, she wasn't sure what she should say to them—what she dared say to them! To tell the truth must be the only way, but she didn't know how much they could take.

When she remembered Paul, it was like a great light at the end of a dark tunnel. Why hadn't she thought of him immediately? She must go to him and ask his advice. When he learned what had happened, he would know exactly what to do. Mark was a dear, but he lacked his brother's decisiveness. If she went to Mark she could imagine his confusion would be as great as her own.

Half an hour later, pretending she had to do some shopping, she rang for a taxi. She had been in touch with Paul and he had agreed to see her, arranging to meet her at his apartment. When she had said she could come to his office, he had replied that he was just leaving. As it was after five, she realised he might be.

She had forgotten about the time, but sitting in the taxi she noticed the shadows were lengthening. The October days were drawing in, it was later than she had thought. No wonder Mrs Finn had looked surprised when she had told her she was going shopping!

Numbly she glanced in the large shoulder-bag she was carrying, making sure everything she needed was there. There was only a few cosmetics, a change of clothing and her night things. She didn't think she was entitled to remain at Coombe Park any longer, unless perhaps Paul advised her to. She wanted to do what he thought best for his parents, and they were her sole consideration at the moment. Once she was assured they weren't too hurt and could manage without her, she would set about finding work immediately. Meanwhile, she had thought it might be wiser to come prepared. If Paul decided it was better that she stayed away from Coombe Park until he broke the news and saw how his parents reacted, she might ask if she could use his apartment for the night. Surely he wouldn't refuse until she discovered if her old room at the flat was still vacant?

Aware that she was in danger of breaking down from sheer nerves, as the taxi dropped her outside the building where Paul lived Jane did her best to control a sense of rising panic. Paul would help her, she kept reiterating, wondering where all her former certainty had fled to. She stared upwards, waves of icy coldness washing over her, making her approach to the glossy, modern vestibule something less than confident.

The commissionaire checked and she was given permission to go up. He smiled, but glanced at her closely, and she guessed she looked pale. Noiselessly the lift swished her to Paul's floor. He was waiting for her as the lift stopped. The doors slid open and he stepped back to allow her out, his face expressionless.

In his apartment he took her coat, bringing her a drink after telling her curtly to sit down. 'To what do I owe the honour of this visit?' he asked, with discouraging formality, placing the drink in her trembling hands.

It was an almost exact repeat of the other evening, she thought, gripping the glass tightly, only then his manner had been pleasanter. Suddenly she was not at all sure she had done the right thing in coming here. Staring apprehensively at his uncompromising features, she found her mindless panic returning again, her body seized by some nameless terror.

Without preamble, she found herself gasping, 'My memory's come back. It happened quite suddenly, this afternoon.'

Paul tensed, staring at her, his eyes chilling with distrust. 'You've been in touch with my parents?'

Naturally they would be his first consideration. 'No,' she seemed to have to use force to get even that word out, 'I had to see you first . . .'

'Why?'

His stinging query made her flinch. 'I—I've discovered I'm not Colin's wife.'

'I know,' he smiled savagely. 'I've known for a while.'

'You do—you did——' she stammered irrationally, feeling stunned as his teeth snapped shut like a steel trap. She wasn't sure what else to say. He was so grimly unsmiling, her voice dried up. Perhaps there was nothing more to say? Perhaps that was all that was necessary?

'I—I'm sorry I deceived . . .'

'Colin?' he rapped.

'No,' she gazed at him helplessly, her eyes fixed on his hard, cruel mouth. 'Your—parents.'

'You're despicable, aren't you!'

Was she? She bit her lip, her eyes nervously dilating, shifting slightly. Possibly she was? Paul wouldn't accuse lightly. It was possible she hadn't wanted to remember, to return to the bleakness of her life before she had met him. It wasn't unknown.

'I'm sorry,' she whispered, shivering, a sob in her throat. 'I wish you'd told me.'

His eyes leaping with fire, he looked down at her. 'Don't you think I wanted to? If I'd had my own way, I would have done! Personally I don't believe a girl like you deserves any kind of consideration, but your doctors warned it could be fatal. And if I ever swing for anyone it's not going to be for a tramp like you! God knows I tried hard enough to get you to betray yourself.'

Jane was white, her blue eyes dark with pain in her tormented face. 'By making love to me?'

'Yes,' he snarled indifferently, then, 'When did you say your memory was supposed to return?'

'This afternoon.'

Suddenly he grabbed her, sending the glass spinning from her nerveless fingers. In a sudden vicious movement his hands twisted in her hair, pulling her head round. She gave a sort of choked scream as his lips crushed hers in utter savagery while his hands explored the tense curves of her breasts. There was no gentleness in his touch, but he made her body yield as helplessly as her mouth.

When he thrust her away, he stared at her, noting, with apparent satisfaction, the tears running down her cheeks, the way in which she was swaying on her feet.

'Well, you lying, cheating little bitch,' he bit out, 'you've had your fun! I suppose you imagined I would welcome you with open arms? Perhaps that's why you pretended to recover. You didn't think you were getting anywhere fast enough!'

Wet-eyed, shaking, Jane tugged at the rings on her finger. Paul was livid, his face black with rage, the dark red blood under his cheekbones adding to his frightening pagan appearance. She didn't want to look at him. All she wanted to do was get away from him. To think he had known all the time and never said anything!

Blindly she pushed the rings in his hands. 'I'm leaving them. I've no right to them—I never had.'

'How true!' he sneered, thrusting them in his pocket.

'I'm going now.' She swallowed convulsively.

He traced the movement in her white throat with stony eyes. 'Where?'

'A flat.'

'Belonging to some of your villainous friends, no doubt, waiting for the spoils you hoped to receive? Give

me your address,' he said curtly. 'I'll see you get
something, otherwise they might wring your pretty little
neck. After all,' cynically he took Colin's rings from his
pocket, jangling them contemplatively, 'I suppose you
could always have sold these.'

'I just took them on impulse,' she cried helplessly.
'He—he did ask me . . .'

'Spare me!' Paul rasped harshly, his face furious
again.

Sobbing, Jane turned from him, running towards the
door.

'Your address!' He hurtled after her, his hard body
tuned for instant action with its amazing vitality.

He caught her at the lift doors as they opened, but
she wrenched from the steely hand on her shoulder. 'I
wouldn't touch a penny of yours!' she gasped, taking
one last look at his dark, handsome face before diving
into the lift and shooting downwards.

She was shaking uncontrollably, a wild trembling
that shook her whole body. Her head ached, her
forehead burned, but, overall, she felt icy cold. What
had Paul meant by villainous friends? She only had
Beth, who could never be classed as such in any way.
The commissionaire glanced at her curiously again, but
she walked straight past him when he asked if she
would like him to get her a taxi.

'No, thank you,' she managed to gulp. She had about
five pounds in small change, she couldn't afford taxis.

The shock of Paul's reception added to the one she
had already received when her memory returned had
her swaying, but she dared not collapse until she found
somewhere to stay for the night. Standing in the street,
her head bent to the now steadily falling rain, mercifully
she was in too numbed a state to be conscious yet of
any real pain. That would come later, when Paul's
rejection and contempt really hit her.

After a few moments she felt sufficiently recovered to
find her way to the nearest underground and take a tube

to the station nearest where she used to live. The area she made for differed dramatically from the one she had just left and Coombe Park, but she was too distraught to give it a thought. Hurrying along, Jane scarcely noticed. She was too wet and unhappy to think of anything but the plight she was in.

Automatically, her feet led her to the shabby street where she found the flat. It was on the ground floor of a house badly in need of a coat of paint and other repairs, with nothing to recommend it other than that it provided shelter from the street.

Having lived here for nearly two years, the first few months of her working life having been spent in a hostel, Jane was indifferent to its poverty-stricken appearance. Beth, who had been in the orphanage with her, and shared the flat with her and another girl, would be married now and probably living in Scotland with her husband. She wasn't sure if Pat, the other girl, would still be here, but there was only one way to find out. Forcing herself forward, Jane entered the peeling entrance hall and knocked on the door of the flat.

The girl who answered her knock uttered a terrified cry and thrust a hand over her mouth when she saw Jane. She went quite pale, looking ready to faint, her eyes wide with alarm. Jane spoke quickly, realising the shock Pat must have received. People didn't usually return from the dead.

'I'm sorry, Pat. Believe me, if I wasn't in such a fix I would have found a way of breaking this to you more gently.'

'Jane, is it really you?' The other girl was obviously shocked and stunned. As Jane nodded, she appeared to regain some composure, but she continued to stare as if she couldn't wholly trust her own eyesight.

'I can explain,' again Jane spoke quickly.

Pat said awkwardly, and Jane caught a note of reluctance, 'I suppose you'd better come in.'

Not exactly a warm welcome, but Jane decided she

couldn't really expect her to be overjoyed. She might have made other arrangements, and she was as white as though she had seen a ghost.

'I'm sorry, Pat,' she reiterated as the door closed behind them and they stood looking at each other in the small kitchen, 'I would have spared you this if I could.'

'But what happened?' Pat exclaimed incredulously. 'You were coming home for Beth's wedding and the plane crashed. We thought you were . . .'

'I know,' Jane said gently. 'It was a mix-up of identities, I'm afraid.' Somehow, as Pat wilted, a little of her own strength returned, but she felt strangely unwilling to go into details. 'I lost my memory and was mistaken for another girl. I believed I was someone else until I recovered and remembered who I really was. I've been in hospital.'

'Good heavens, all this time!'

Jane suddenly decided not to correct this impression. She couldn't bear to to talk about the Denyers, and Pat would be curious. Well, who wouldn't be?

'Yes,' she said. 'And I'm terribly sorry about Beth's wedding.'

'Yes,' Pat sounded dazed. 'It spoiled her day. She cried something awful!'

'It must have done.' Jane swallowed tears of regret from her throat.

'She's not here now,' the awkward expression returned to Pat's face. 'She went back north with Tom.'

'To the Shetlands? Well, she would, wouldn't she? She was so thrilled when Tom got a house.'

Pat shrugged, fast recovering her equilibrium, which was never easily dented. 'She seems happy enough now—I had a card.'

Jane tried to smile, but began feeling dizzy again and was forced to sit down. Pat didn't ask her to, but Jane thought nothing of it, not until a few minutes later. The three girls had shared the only other room in the flat. It was large, they had each had a single bed and it doubled as a lounge, of sorts, during the day.

'Pat,' she said tentatively, 'I realise you might have new flatmates, but would it be all right if I stayed for the night? I wouldn't mind sleeping on the floor.'

Pat stared at her in dismay. 'I'm not sure,' she began. 'No!' she said more firmly, 'I'm afraid you can't.' As Jane stared back at her in silent bewilderment, she flushed with embarrassment and tried to explain. 'You see, after Beth went and I thought you weren't coming back, I—er—well, Jack moved in.'

'Oh, I see.' All too clearly, Jane did. She felt a flicker of distaste, although it was only over herself she was usually straitlaced, Paul being the only man to whom she had ever been tempted to surrender her chastity. A lot of couples lived together for various reasons which was no one's business but their own. It wasn't that Pat was living wth someone that Jane objected to, it was because the man was Jack Adams. He would think nothing of making love to Pat with an audience looking on. He was coarse and nasty, there were no other words to describe him. Beth and she had often wondered whatever Pat saw in him.

Jane's face flushed. 'Don't worry, Pat—I shouldn't dream of playing gooseberry. I'll find something and come back tomorrow for my things.'

'Oh,' Pat was embarrassed again, 'I'm afraid I threw most of your things out. That is, I gave them to the charity shop down the road. Beth thought it was best, after she was married and we didn't think you would want them any more.'

'I understand, Pat,' Jane broke in, knowing she might have done the same thing herself, and trying not to notice that Pat was wearing what had once been her best sweater.

'If you can't get in anywhere, give me a ring,' Pat called after her as she left.

It would be a waste of time, Jane thought with a

mirthless smile as she retraced her steps along the street. Pat, like Paul, had clearly no wish to see her again.

In the end she had to spend the night in a hostel. It was unavoidable as she couldn't afford anything else, but she was grateful to have any kind of roof over her head. By the time she settled in, she was feeling so terrible she feared she might break down, and was relieved that the series of shocks she had received that day appeared to have frozen her ability to weep, so she was in no danger of disturbing the other girls with whom she shared the hostel's humble facilities. They were mostly, she gathered, girls who had come to London seeking work—or who had found work but not a room. She could see they were, on the whole, too preoccupied with their own problems to concern themselves over-much with hers.

Throughout the night, Jane lay trying not to think of her warm bed and lovely room at Coombe Park. It was the first room of her own she had ever known, her recollections of the house she had lived in with her parents being now very dim. She thought of the Denyers, their kindness, all they had done for her, but her gratitude, compassion and love she trained solely on Mary, John and Mark.

She could only think of Paul with bitterness. How could he believe she had deliberately set out to deceive any of them? He hadn't even asked for her side of the story. He was convinced she had posed as his brother's wife in the hope of securing a fortune. Although the hospital had advised him against confronting her, he had obviously been sure her amnesia wasn't genuine, and because of this his hate and contempt had increased daily, driving her relentlessly to drastic lengths. He had taken her out and made love to her, clearly with the intention of tricking her into betraying herself, and for that, Jane knew, she would never forgive him!

CHAPTER FIVE

JANE didn't wake up the next morning, because she had never been asleep. Heavy eyed she managed to swallow a cup of tea but couldn't face the rest of her breakfast. After paying the small amount asked for accommodation, she decided to call on the agency to see if there was any chance of getting any of the fee she had never received from the Italian job. She was broke and it seemed her only hope, although she doubted if she was legally entitled to anything after all this time.

Glancing in a mirror at her ravaged face, she feared her chances of pursuing a modelling career might be nil. Clare Farrage, who ran the modelling agency which had previously given her work, was brilliant to the extent of rarely putting a foot wrong, but Jane viewed her own future bleakly as she left the hostel to catch a bus.

When Clare saw her she looked nearly as alarmed as Pat had done, but because the nature of her business had, over the years, made her less vulnerable to shock, she recovered more quickly.

After Jane had made another brief explanation, she smiled grimly. 'I should be inured to such things, heaven knows! If I didn't have the resilience of a stone wall, I'd never survive. It's nice to have you back, dear despite the rather shattering circumstances—although,' she subjected Jane to a much closer scrutiny, 'I can't see you being able to work for a while.'

Jane assured her that she was really quite fit while admitting that the shock of her memory returning had set her back a bit. Then she took a deep breath and asked about the money she was owed. 'If I'm not entitled to it now, I quite understand,' she said.

Clare had a reputation for treating her girls right if

they did right by her, a reputation she guarded
jealously. 'The money's still here, dear. We always
retain a fee for a while, for several reasons.' For the
Italian job she quoted an extremely nice sum, advising
Jane to take it and find a quiet resort for a week or so,
until she recovered.

'Come back and see me then,' she said, 'and I'll see
what I can do.'

Jane was reluctant to follow Clare's advice until she
took time to think about it and realised it was sound.
She found a cheap boarding-house on the South Coast
and within a few days at least began to look better. She
spent long hours walking by the sea, breathing the
crisply reviving October air and trying not to worry over
much about Mary and John Denyer and the additional
burden of unhappiness they must now be having to bear.

When she returned to London, Clare was pleased
with her—and she had news for her. Some old friends
of hers had an attic room going spare, if Jane wanted
it.

'They'll be mother and father to you,' she warned as
Jane accepted gratefully. 'And don't thank me,' she
hastened to add, as Jane began to overwhelmingly. 'It
just happened to come up and I thought of you. This
doesn't mean that I've suddenly decided you're the
discovery of the year!'

This appeared depressingly true in the days that
followed, but if no actual modelling work was available,
Clare asked her to do a few hours' typing now and
again. This, with the residue of her savings, kept her
going, and after completing such formalities as re-
establishing her identity with the authorities, she settled
down as patiently as she could to wait.

She did, in fact, appreciate the chance to regain her
old office skills, for she knew even if she did make a
success of modelling it was a short career at its best. She
actually put her name down at the nearest unemploy-
ment exchange for work as a secretary, but was told

that until the present recession was over there was little chance of her finding such a position.

The first modelling job she did was for tights. 'You've got about the most beautiful legs on my books,' Clara shrugged, 'so you may as well have it.' After this there were two more for the same thing, then it was back to typing again.

Jane was working in the office the morning the call came from International, one of the biggest, some said the biggest, advertising agencies in the country. She put it through to Clare herself.

'Okay, okay, okay!' through the open door of Clare's office which was rarely closed, she heard Clare impatiently replying. 'Of course I won't let you down. Have I ever?

'Oh, lord!' she sighed, coming off the phone. 'Sometimes I think I'll get myself a job where people aren't so hard to please. Can you beat it! Six girls I sent them yesterday and none will do. They want six more by this afternoon.'

She had left her chair and was leaning on the door between the two rooms as she spoke. Jane could tell she was anxious. She was beginning to recognise that when Clare's superb Oxford confidence was shaken there was a problem. 'Trouble?' she asked tentatively.

'The trouble is,' Clare exclaimed angrily, 'the girls I sent yesterday were my best! Where do I find six better?'

Jane could see her dilemma. 'Who's being so choosey, or shouldn't I ask?'

'Oh, you may ask, but even if I knew I wouldn't be allowed to say. It's a giant cosmetic firm, but these sort of things are very hush-hush. Their products are always the best and they insist on the best to advertise them. They want a girl not only with delicate looks but with a delicate air, and it appears that none of the girls I've sent so far have it!'

As Jane could think of no constructive comment to

make, Clare obviously believed she didn't understand the situation. 'You know the sort of thing they're thinking of—a kind of Jeannie, with light brown hair, floating like ... Oh, Jane!' she interrupted herself, alarmed, 'what have I said? You've gone quite white!'

'Nothing you said,' Jane mumbled, staring helplessly down at her desk. It was sheer coincidence that Paul Denyer had said much the same thing.

'I should send you,' normally Clare would have insisted on knowing what was wrong, but her own immediate problem loomed larger than any other and the sight of Jane's pale face had given her an idea. 'You're lovely enough and you've got brown hair and your paleness certainly gives you a delicate air. It's a kind of promotion job, usually lasting a few months, but actually,' she frowned, 'I don't think you'd have the stamina.'

'I'm really quite recovered,' said Jane, pushing all thought of Paul Denyer from her mind and somehow welcoming the idea of being able to work until she was too tired to think. It was unlikely that she would even be considered though as she was practically unknown.

Clare seemed to think it unlikely, too, if she was too kind to say so outright. 'You can always go along to make up the numbers, I suppose,' she pondered. 'Regardless of their client, I can't afford to offend International, they put quite a lot of bread and butter my way. Now, let's see if we can rake up another five.'

Jane hadn't time to go home and find something really smart to wear, as a relatively quiet morning changed into something approaching pandemonium. Clare had plenty of girls on her books, but they had great difficulty in contacting all of those she considered might be suitable. In the end, Jane had to make do with the dress she had on, a thin silk, which she wore in the office because Clare liked the heating full on.

'Never mind,' Clare's full-time secretary whispered sympathetically, 'pale green suits you, you look wonderful, and you never know,' she laughed, 'in this game anything can happen!'

After lunch Jane and the five other young women whom Clare had managed to round up arrived in a flurry at the headquarters of International. Jane, breathlessly bringing up the rear, tried to make herself invisible as they were met by a tall young man who drawled sarcastically, 'Is this the best Clare can do?'

'Accounts executive, one of them!' Lena, the girl beside Jane, muttered. 'Swine!'

Jane gulped as another girl, ignoring the young man's remark, asked him sharply, 'What was wrong with Somalia? She's the top.'

'As well as being very—er—friendly with one of your directors,' someone else chimed in, in a carrying whisper.

The young man treated them both to a lofty glance. 'That's just it, isn't it?' he retorted coolly. 'She's too well known.'

'Come on, girls, we may as well go home,' jeered a beautiful blonde, but Jane noticed no one moved.

As the interviewing began and she waited her turn, Jane thought of the girls she had met since starting to work for Clare. They were a mixed bunch, hardworking, ambitious and mostly goodhumoured, willing to do anyone a good turn. It was only a few, she reflected, who were really mercenary and acquired a bad reputation. What people tended to forget was that most professions had an equal share of these.

She was last to go in; Clare had told her to be. 'They'll probably choose Lena,' she said, 'so if you let her and the others go first, it's unlikely they'll want to see you.'

Clare was concerned for her, Jane knew, she hadn't meant to be unflattering. Unfortunately, judging from the sullen expression on Lena's face when she returned, she had been rejected. So, it seemed, were the others. Jane departed, her confidence in her own chances very low indeed and looking incredibly nervous.

'You're not being interviewed for some cannibalistic banquet, darling,' the accounts executive snapped, looking fed up to the teeth but determined. Then his manner suddenly changed as Jane swept him a mutely appealing glance. Something about her appeared to bring a rather startled gleam of surprise to his eyes, but before he could co-ordinate his apparently shattered thoughts, they had traversed the length of a passage and entered a room full of people. At least to Jane it seemed full of people.

The head of the famous firm of luxurious, fabulously expensive cosmetics, took one long look at her and, to everyone's obvious relief, decided immediately she would do. Olive Frey clapped her hands excitedly when Jane appeared and declared she was exactly the kind of girl she had been searching for. As she was renowned for her business acumen as well as her instant impeccable judgment, no one seemed the least inclined to question her decision. Jane wondered if she was the only one to believe Mrs Frey might have been too hasty.

Bewildered, she listened to Olive Frey, noting each of her individual features separately, pointing out why she considered Jane's face would make a perfect medium for advertising cosmetics. Such phrases as 'eyes like violets drenched in rain—skin like silk' flowed enthusiastically. Jane scarcely recognised herself and flushed with embarrassment, but as colour crept to her cheeks it merely brought forth more satisfied exclamations.

There was more talk, a lot of it, as Jane was turned round and round, inspected and discussed as though she was some inanimate object. No one was actively unkind. Olive, who hadn't given the young executive a chance to make proper introductions, eventually asked Jane's name, then introduced her to those members of her staff who were with her. She seemed warmhearted and cheerful, but she clearly regarded Jane as a piece of valuable merchandise whose face was going to prove a great asset in boosting her new and so far secret range of skin products.

When Mrs Frey began murmuring about getting contracts drawn up, Jane was jerked abruptly from the rather incredulous daze she was in as she suddenly realised what she might be letting herself in for. She recognised she was being given an opportunity which would make most other girls green with envy, but she was unable to disregard an inexplicable weight of apprehension.

She was waiting for an opportunity to speak, which wasn't easy above the constant babble of voices, when Mrs Frey broke in with a query that startled her afresh.

'Where's Mark got to?' she exclaimed. 'The naughty man promised he'd be here!'

'Just arriving. He was held up,' the young executive, obviously praying, explained breathlessly. Mrs Frey, everyone knew, was notorious for changing her mind. She looked satisfied this time, but if she felt slighted in any way she was quite capable of walking out. His sigh of relief was clearly audible as the door opened and the chairman's brother appeared.

No one noticed Jane looking ready to faint. She went pale, her eyes staring. She had been standing, but she sank in the chair which was luckily pressing the backs of her legs. What a fool she had been not to have guessed that International was the huge advertising network belonging to the Denyer family!

'Mark, I've decided!' Olive Frey cried before he had scarcely got a foot through the door. 'Such a beautiful girl—I'm enchanted! You're always so clever at finding me exactly what I want.'

No one suggested it had been a close thing. It would have been a waste of breath anyway, but they were all too busy wondering why Mark should be gazing at Jane with such stunned surprise in his eyes. She was, as Olive had said, enchanting, or she would be before Olive had finished with her, but surely Denyer met girls like her every day?

Mark, as if realising himself how his attitude was arousing curiosity, replied jerkily, 'If you're sure?'

'Of course I'm sure!' Olive positively bridled. 'Jane is exactly what I want, and if you want my account, Mark, have a contract drawn up immediately. With this girl and good media planning, our new spring range will be unbeatable!'

Jane had suffered shock when her memory returned, but this was worse. She had had no idea that this was a Denyer agency. Until now she had had little contact with such places or the firms whose products she indirectly helped to sell. She had once met the advertising manager of a large company who ran their own advertising department as part of the overall marketing set-up, but that was all. Most organisations preferred to delegate this function to the experts, the advertising agencies which employed a complete battery of specialists in design, copy-writing and research. Usually if a model was engaged she only saw a photographer, and the weary hours spent posing in a thousand different positions could be very tiring. Even finding the right kind of smile could take half a day.

Most modelling sessions were over in a day, though, apart from perhaps clothes, especially in a foreign country, which could take weeks. This job for Mrs Frey suggested something different again, and if it meant running into Paul Denyer, that wasn't something Jane was prepared to risk.

'Don't I have any say in the matter?' she asked the young executive still bending over her, in a hoarse whisper.

'Not if you know what's good for you, darling,' he muttered, squashing her protests with a glance which both threatened and begged.

'Did you wish to say something, Miss—er—Carey?' Mark's voice was unfamiliarly curt as his eyes quickly skimmed the sheet of paper a secretary thrust in his hands.

'I'd like to speak to you alone,' Jane replied faintly.

'Later,' he dismissed her faltering request, obviously as irrelevant. Appearing to pull himself together, he turned to Olive. 'This calls for drinks, don't you think? If you'd all like to step into my office?'

They went to the next floor, but through his office to a room which was clearly part of a private suite used for entertaining top clients. The room was large and luxuriously furnished as well as being quiet and secluded. Jane wondered if Paul brought his lady friends here. Mark, she remembered, had once said Paul was no monk, but rarely allowed the women he knew to encroach on his private and personal life.

There was plenty to drink, spirits and wine flowing in abundance. Mark, if not as brilliant and assertive as his brother, had been well and cleverly tutored. Keeping a firm hold of Jane's arm, he waited until Mrs Frey had downed her third gin and tonic, then began talking.

'I'll get on to our legal department straight away. If you do the same we should have contracts drawn up ready to sign in a day or two.'

Olive nodded with a satisfied beam. 'When's Paul due back?'

'I'm not sure,' Mark frowned as Jane paled. 'Any time now.'

I have to ring Clare, Jane thought in panic, I can't do this! Mark must know it wasn't possible! She couldn't face Paul again, although she almost wished he had been here. If he had been here he would have had her thrown out long before things had reached this stage. If it was a humiliation she couldn't bear thinking of, it would have saved her a lot more pain in the long run.

Feeling she had suffered enough at his hands, she asked to be excused a minute. The excited babble of conversation barely paused. She was merely told not to be long.

Next door to Mark's office she found another that appeared deserted. Too upset to wonder if her conduct was ethical, Jane dived in and closed the door. Picking up the phone, she dialled Clare's number.

Clare answered herself, to Jane's relief. 'I can't do it!' she cried, before Clare could speak.

'Nonsense!' Clare exclaimed, after demanding and being given a less than convincing explanation, Jane having suddenly discovered the real truth impossible to relate. 'Olive Frey is the chance of a lifetime, love, and not only for you.'

'But . . .' Jane began desperately.

'No buts!' Clare retorted angrily, cutting her off.

Jane dropped her receiver miserably. It was hopeless, Clare wasn't even willing to discuss it, and how could she let her down? She owed Clare so much. Hadn't she helped her when she didn't seem to have a friend in the world? She drew a trembling breath as she reluctantly returned to the other room again. Whatever was asked of her she would have to go through with it. It seemed she had no alternative.

Half an hour later everyone had gone and she was alone at last with Mark.

'I . . .' they both began together.

'Jane,' Mark pushed on as she paused, 'let me speak. I'm sorry if I was distant in front of the others, but I got a hell of a shock. When I saw you I nearly dropped!'

'I'm sorry,' Jane muttered, ready to burst into tears.

'I'd no idea you were a model, for one thing,' Mark mumbled, his former decisiveness deserting him and looking as if he didn't know what to say.

'I've only done a few jobs,' she gazed at him more hopefully, 'which is why I don't think this is a good idea. I'm really a secretary.'

'Not any more you aren't,' he replied absently, placing another drink in her hands.

Jane wanted to argue, but suddenly there were more

important things. Mark knew it too, only, like her, he didn't know where to begin. She took a gulp of her drink, searching for a little Dutch courage. 'Mark,' she asked, 'how are your parents?'

'Bearing up, but they've been through a tough time, what with one thing and another.'

She could guess what he meant by that!

'Jane,' Mark suddenly burst out, his pleasant face unusually drawn, 'we still don't understand exactly what happened. Won't you tell me?'

'Didn't Paul?' she asked bitterly.

'He told us so much,' Mark replied tensely, 'but since the police contacted us and we were told you were a single girl of twenty-one and never had been Colin's wife, he won't hear your name mentioned. I think he's as confused as the rest of us.'

Jane felt confused too. 'What did he say, after I'd gone, that is?'

'He said you'd called at his apartment after having recovered your memory and you'd admitted that you hadn't been married to Colin.'

'He said he already knew,' she broke in. 'I didn't wonder how—I simply imagined he hadn't told me for fear of possible repercussions.'

'He learnt when he went to Italy—remember that trip?' as Jane nodded numbly, Mark went on, 'He discovered enough over there to be totally convinced you'd married Colin bigamously, hoping to get money out of him in order to set up in business with your real husband. He came back flaming mad, apparently, but your doctors absolutely forbade a confrontation.'

'We must have been talking at cross-purposes,' Jane breathed in horror. 'He gave every indication of knowing the true story, so I didn't think it necessary to explain. Especially as he wouldn't listen. He was furious, but I thought it was because he believed I'd been deliberately deceiving your parents for what I could get out of them.'

'Oh, God!' Mark groaned, his eyes full of compassion. 'What a muddle!'

'Do your parents and Paul feel any better about me, now they've learned the truth?' she faltered shakily. Somehow it was desperately important that they should.

'My parents do.' Mark hesitated as Jane clutched his arm without realising what she was doing. 'Since they learned that you were just a single girl, they've been doing everything they can to find you, but I'm afraid Paul's still suspicious.'

'Suspicious?' Jane went white. She disliked Paul Denyer, despised him for having hounded her from the beginning, behind the pretence of friendship. Now she hated him. 'Why is he still suspicious?' she gasped.

Again mark hesitated, clearly embarrassed, but the intentness of Jane's wide-eyed glance compelled him to confess.

'Because of the rings. You were wearing Colin's rings—his signet one with his initials, which he had obviously used for a wedding ring, couldn't be mistaken.'

Jane felt completely stunned. If it had been established beyond all doubt that she'd had nothing to do with Colin, how had they imagined she had come to be in possession of his rings? She tried to put herself in their position and her mind boggled.

'Oh, Mark,' she exclaimed, tears in her eyes, 'I never realised!'

All at once she began telling Mark everything. About the modelling trip to the Italian resort, her hasty return for Beth's wedding and having to sit beside his brother and his wife on the plane. She told him about the other girl being called Jane, too, and of the way she had gone on.

'Your brother couldn't seem to control her,' she said. 'She kept demanding money and threatening him. By the time we were due to land she was quite hysterical, to the extent of ordering me to wear her rings. I wouldn't have done so if Colin hadn't begged me to, for just a few minutes until he got her calmed down. I was actually taking them off again when something terrible appeared to happen. I don't remember any more.'

'Oh, darling!' Mark groaned, gathering her close as if trying to shield her from remembered horror. 'It must have been a terrible situation to be in, and we all misjudged you.'

'I can understand how it happened.' Jane clung to him for a moment, giving in to an overwhelming desire for comfort. 'I felt sorry for Colin.'

'He got in touch with Paul, the day before he and this girl whom he thought was his wife left Italy. His marriage wasn't working out, he said he was coming home. He was clearly distracted and asked for Paul's help. Paul promised to be at the airport to meet him.'

'It adds up.' Reflective and distressed, Jane gently freed herself from Mark's arms. It seemed scarcely the time to wonder why his closeness didn't affect her the way Paul's did.

Reluctantly Mark let her go. 'My mother was convinced there must be a good explanation, so did Dad. I did too, of course.'

'But not Paul?'

Mark stirred awkwardly, then he shrugged. 'You know how he's inclined to be cynical.'

Jane let this pass. Paul was altogether harder and tougher than Mark. He was a mixture of steel and cast-iron, while the blood in his veins was hot. Jane flushed, hating to recall her own experience of it. 'It doesn't matter,' she replied hastily. Perhaps Paul's blood was just as cool as the rest of him. Hadn't he told her himself that he had merely pretended passion as a means of helping her to remember?

'My parents will be enormously relieved to know you are at least safe and well,' Mark was saying. 'You'll have to come to dinner at Coombe Park. Even the dogs are missing you!'

'I'd love to,' she said, knowing she never would. Somehow she couldn't bear to. If she was given a definite invitation she would have to find an excuse. She had tasted family life for a few weeks, going back would be too painful. 'I'll give your mother a ring some time,' she said. 'I must apologise for leaving so suddenly, but I expect Paul explained.'

Mark smiled grimly, and she guessed Paul's explanation hadn't been exactly charitable.

As he nodded, she looked at him anxiously. 'You must see now why I don't want to do this thing for Mrs Frey? Anyway, Paul wouldn't have me.'

'He never lets anything interfere with business!' Mark protested in alarm. 'He'd skin me alive if I let you go. Besides, once I've told him what happened on the plane he can't have anything to hold against you.'

'But I have against him!' Jane was suddenly angry.

'I realise he can be pretty frightening when he feels like it,' Mark's pleasant face darkened as if he recalled instances when it had happened to him, 'but he never bears a grudge.'

Jane's soft lips tightened. People who walked relentlessly over the feelings of others rarely did. They prided themselves on their forgiving nature, forgetting it was they who should be looking for forgiveness, not their poor victims.

The trouble was Mark didn't know the half of it, and she couldn't tell him. 'I don't think I can forget the things he said,' she hedged. 'It wouldn't make for a good working relationship.'

'You wouldn't see him, though, he's away a lot,' Mark declared, going quite pale. 'Jane, you have to be sensible and I have to persuade you, no matter what it takes.' He looked ready to go down on his hands and knees. 'Look at it this way. If you absolutely refuse to do this job, Olive Frey would take her account elsewhere. And although we hate losing anyone it wouldn't be a major calamity. At least, we'd certainly survive—but would you? Clare Farrage would see you never got the chance of another job. She's a very warmhearted lady, but she can be extremely vindictive. She would blacklist you, and I'm not sure you wouldn't deserve it.'

'J-just because I don't want to take everything I'm offered?' Jane stammered.

'No, because in this case you feel like being a little coward. You're indulging yourself, at the risk of upsetting countless people, merely because you don't feel you can face Paul.'

'That's not true!' she denied.

'Isn't it?'

For a fleeting moment he resembled Paul so much she trembled. He was right, of course, and in the end she gave in, unable to argue against such crafty logic. She couldn't bear to think of herself as without courage, or to be branded a coward. She hated Paul Denyer, she told herself thickly, and hate should be all the defence she required. She wasn't vulnerable any more, if she remembered that she should be quite safe, she had nothing to fear. It was maddening to find, after reaching such sane conclusions, that on first seeing Paul again she felt like running a mile!

It happened three days later when the contracts were being signed. Once this was done, everyone drank to the success of Olive Frey's new enterprise, the entire team pledging their co-operation. Jane was being made such a fuss of it was beginning to go to her head. She wasn't used to so much champagne, so many flattering remarks. In time it had a drugging effect stronger than the disturbing thoughts she was just managing to keep at bay. She didn't even notice Mark's unsuccessful attempts to get a word alone with her. Deliberately, still feeling a little resentful towards him, she looked at him as little as possible.

She regretted this, five minutes later when Paul appeared and she understood what Mark had been trying to tell her.

She went so pale that Olive glanced at her with concern. 'I think Jane needs some air,' she exclaimed. 'She looks quite overcome!'

Jane could have murdered her, for as everyone obligingly fell back, Paul shot through the resulting gap. Coolly authoritative, he bent over Olive's hand, the grey eyes he raised to her face as he straightened amused and faintly mocking. 'It appears you've done it again,' he smiled.

Olive's positive shriek of delight was heard by all. 'Paul I knew you would make it.'

'For you,' Paul grinned, 'it was worth the effort.'

No other man, Jane fumed, would get away with half as much flattery he obviously didn't mean. Keeping her eyes averted, she tried not to see the gleam of his thick dark hair, the curl of his mouth, the hard strength of his whole face.

'I like to see a woman satisfied,' he was retorting blandly. 'It increases my own pleasure.'

How could he! Jane wondered, delicate colour tinting her cheeks.

Olive laughed, completely relaxed as Paul cleverly talked her language. He often seemed the only person in the world who remembered that before she had met and married her late husband and took over the running of his business, she had been a strip-tease artist. Often she wondered what had happened to that girl, under the subsequent smother of respectability, and was glad when Paul occasionally reminded her. If only she had been ten years younger than him instead of ten years older, then little girls like this model his eyes were resting on so speculatively wouldn't have stood a chance!

With a sigh she got down to business again 'You're quite right, Paul, I am extremely satisfied more so than I've been for a long time. Do you know Jane?'

He bowed slightly, not offering his hand or kissing hers as he had done Olive's. 'I believe I've had the pleasure, although I might have mixed her up with someone else.'

'I was thrilled when I found her.' To Jane's embarrassment, Olive again began listing what she considered her good points while Paul listened so attentively that no one but herself might have guessed his underlying contempt.

Someone brought him a drink, seeming to know his tastes as he swallowed the double whisky neat. As Olive paused for breath, he said idly, 'When Mark rang me yesterday in L.A., I thought he was exaggerating. It seemed a good idea to come and see for myself. A client like you isn't easily deceived, but it has been known to happen.'

Olive, obviously preening that she should be receiving such attention from a man whose reputation and achievement in advertising was so brilliant, was actually heard to ask if he agreed with her choice.

Jane, despite her growing antagonism, felt a flicker of frustration when he merely nodded indifferently.

Olive, too, must have been a little put out at such a lack of enthusiasm, for she said stubbornly, 'With my help, Jane's going to be a sensation.'

Jane shuddered inwardly as the grey eyes travelled over her, narrowed and sardonic. 'I'm sure she'll co-operate if you've that in mind,' he drawled suavely.

Jane could have wept with relief when the session was over, but not when Mark whispered that Paul wished to see her in his office.

'I—I can't!' she improvised wildly. 'I've got a date.'

'Paul would never listen to an excuse like that.' Mark wore his worried look again, which he usually did when both he and Paul were in the same country, 'For heaven's sake, Jane,' he implored, 'have you forgotten what I told you the other day, about being a coward?'

Jane ignored this, not considering it relevant at the moment. Hadn't she spent the last hour bravely facing Paul, enduring his concealed taunts and continual barrage of mocking glances? Shouldn't Mark perhaps consider following his own advice? With Paul, he was more subservient than a lapdog. Even Olive Frey had noticed it.

'Is it absolutely necessary?' she asked sharply, hoping to persuade him by showing a little aggression, to agreeing it wasn't. 'I've signed a contract, everything's tied up. Surely there can't be anything else?'

Mark merely looked uncomfortable and began muttering about better being safe than sorry. 'I'm sure he won't keep you a minute.'

'What did you say to him yesterday?' She was suddenly, perhaps unfairly suspicious. 'He told Mrs Frey you'd been in touch.'

'I couldn't say much over the phone.' Mark twiddled with a pen he was holding until Jane could have screamed. 'When he asked whom we'd got for the Frey account and I said you, I had to tell him enough to prevent him coming back and throwing you out.'

'He still came back . . .'

Mark frowned. 'Don't ask me why. Beats me.'

'Doesn't he trust your judgment?'

'Not always, Miss Carey,' a voice hit them from behind, from the doorway, shocking them both into whirling around as Paul strode arrogantly into the room.

CHAPTER SIX

MARK might have been an errant schoolboy, the way Paul dismissed him. Then he told Jane to sit down, although he didn't himself. He perched on the edge of the desk, so she had to avert her eyes from the powerful muscles of his thighs which seemed somehow to taunt the cool indifference she pretended. He had been having a priveate word with Olive Frey, and she wondered what they had been talking about.

'I don't know how you have the nerve to order Mark out of his own office!' she exclaimed, raising disdainful brows to stop him guessing she was trembling. 'I think he deserves more consideration.'

His eyes went icy. 'There's obviously something biting you, Miss Carey. I've had a tedious journey and I'm not too happy about what's been going on while I've been away.'

'Mark does his best,' she cut in, quoting his mother.

'Maybe, but I'm not dishing out accolades.'

She hated his arrogance, his unconcealed contempt for those with less confidence than himself. His own personality was pitched to the degree of never puting a foot wrong. He was ruthless in going after what he wanted and getting it and had no sympathy for those who faltered and fell by the wayside. Not even if it happened to be his own brother.

'You use people, don't you!' She didn't try to hide her resentment. 'Even Olive Frey, you flirted with her disgustingly!'

'Miss Carey!'

Regardless of the warning in his voice, she rushed on, 'I was there, you know!'

'So you were.' He stared back at her until she could

almost feel the anger burning through his veins. 'I hope you realise your own good fortune? If I had known you were applying for this job I wouldn't have allowed it.'

Jane shivered, her pale skin flushing scarlet in the face of such open hostility. 'What do you mean?' she whispered. 'You can't still believe what you did about me? Mark said he explained.'

'He did, briefly, although I've yet to decide if you're telling the truth.'

'But it is the truth!' she whispered, her voice throbbing in sick panic.

Paul's eyes glittered menacingly. 'You can take comfort that the authorities have checked you out and are satisfied, but don't expect me to apologise for a situation which might have confused the devil. All the evidence was against you, remember. I still think it is.'

Jane's face was suddenly white. It was obvious he didn't trust her. He was convinced there was something, somewhere which might discredit her completely. 'God, how I hate you!' she breathed, scarcely aware of having spoken aloud until he laughed.

'Perhaps we might find a certain satisfaction in hating each other?' His voice was mocking while no humour touched his darkening glance. Without warning he slid off the desk, jerking her to her feet, his face a contemptuous mask as she stumbled against him. 'Hate is a lot healthier than a pretence of loving, don't you think?'

'I've never pretended to love you.'

He steadied her before thrusting his hands in his pockets. 'At Coombe Park you gave that impression—for some reason.'

As he stared at her coldly, Jane began to realise the depth of his distrust. It could have something to do with the fact that perhaps for once in his life he had been proved wrong, but she didn't doubt it was a force to be reckoned with. Nor did she doubt that Paul could deviously reduce the few months she was contracted to work for Olive Frey to a time of sheer misery. She could feel his silent anger in every nerve of her body.

Blindly she turned from him. 'I'm going home, Mr Denyer.'

'I'll take you.'

'No, thanks!'

'Get your coat.'

Raging, she was just about to protest again when she suddenly decided it wasn't worth it. If she fed his antagonism it might only grow into something more than capable of hurting her. On the way to the car, when he said there were things he wanted to discuss, she merely shrugged carelessly.

He didn't speak until they arrived at the street where she lived and he parked outside the door. It was a long drive and she hoped bitterly that he had enjoyed it, with the evening being so wet and dark. He had the kind of features that betrayed nothing, and she searched in vain for even the faintest indication that he regretted not letting her come home alone.

'Goodnight,' she muttered, on the pavement almost before he stopped.

In a flash he was beside her, leaving her wondering how, for a big man, he could move so quickly. 'Lead on,' he snapped. 'I feel like a cup of coffee or something. We can have it in your room.'

'I'm not allowed men in my flat.' It had never been mentioned, but he wasn't to know that. 'I've no wish to offend my landlord.'

'Leave me to deal with him,' Paul retorted, taking her arm and pushing her forward.

At the top of the tall house where she had three small rooms, Jane left him sitting in the lounge while she went to the tiny kitchen and plugged in the kettle. Returning, minutes later, with two mugs of instant, she placed one, not very graciously in front of him.

'It's the best I can do.' She stared at him defiantly, remaining standing.

'Sit down,' he commanded, for the second time that evening.

When she stayed exactly where she was, he placed a heavy hand on her shoulder, forcing her to change her mind. Before joining her on the couch he looked down at her for a long moment, his mouth compressed.

'Perhaps we'd better get this straight, Miss Carey. As long as you're engaged to work on the Frey account you'll do exactly as I say. I refuse to add to my already heavy work load by having to repeat everything twice before you obey.'

Her blue eyes sparkling with anger, she glared at him. 'That can't apply to my private life.'

'In this case it does,' he replied curtly. 'In a career such as you've chosen, you'll find your working and private life frequently overlap, and you have to abide by the rules.'

Jane said sharply, 'I didn't choose modelling for a career. I'm trained for office work, hasn't Mark told you? I don't believe I'm strictly model material.'

His eyes pinned her against the back of the couch while his lips twisted. 'Are you fishing for compliments? Do you need me to tell you how good you look?'

'No!' she breathed tautly, hating the way his cynical glance was moving over her, 'I don't!'

'Well, make the most of your opportunities while they last,' he jeered. 'The Frey job might lead to some nice fat commissions, if you play your cards right, to say nothing of men.'

'Men?' she echoed.

Paul's voice hardened with contempt. 'For a lot of men the word model is sufficient. Added to your deceptively innocent air with its undoubtedly sexy undertones, you should have no trouble.'

Jane curled her hands to control their itching desire to wipe the mockery off his face. 'I signed a contract for work, Mr Denyer, not for the sale of my—my body to the highest bidder!'

'Time will tell,' he shrugged, clearly inclined to believe his own theories.

Incensed, Jane retorted, 'How I amuse myself after work is none of your business. I'd thank you not to interfere!'

'Lady,' he leaned towards her coolly, 'I'll do all the interfering I want to, and remember, your entire future could depend on me.'

'Because you know the most influential people?'

'Partly.'

Bitterly she glared at him, wondering where the man had gone whom she had clung to for weeks. Or had she merely imagined the comfort of his arms, his kindness? Memories can become twisted, exaggerated. You didn't look too closely into motives when you were ill, especially if it was an illness of the mind. You clung to what you thought was there, and in the hospital Paul had been all that was there. That was where she had made her mistake. He had let her cling, not out of kindness but because he had believed she had been married to his brother. Since he had discovered she wasn't Colin's wife, his charitable feelings had been replaced by contempt. And despite the fact that during that terrible afternoon in his apartment, he had done his brutal best to strip her of any illusions, he was apparently determined to make doubly sure she had none left!

Taking a deep breath, she lowered her eyes, wishing she wasn't so conscious of his masculine strength. 'Is that all, Mr Denyer?'

'Not quite,' he mocked, infuriatingly aware of her attempts to conceal her angry distress. His eyes were trained on her fast beating heart and she could almost feel his derisive amusement. 'How old are you?' he asked abruptly.

He must know, or hadn't the authorities told him? 'Twenty-one,' she replied, disinclined to make a secret of it.

'We have your full particulars,' he assured her. 'I just wanted to make sure.'

The grey eyes were enigmatic as they watched her. She hoped he couldn't see the tension she was experiencing, but something in the cynical twist of his lips made her suspect he knew exactly the way she felt.

'So,' he shrugged at last, just as she was beginning to realise what a worm felt like on the end of a pin, 'where did you go to when you fled from my apartment?'

He had a nerve, mentioning that! 'Back to my old room.'

'Why aren't you still there?'

'Does it matter?' she asked coldly. 'I'd rather not talk about it.'

'Suit yourself,' he muttered absently, letting his narrowed glance wander the length of her slender, seductive figure before returning to the beautifully modelled bones of her face, to rest on her full, sensitive mouth. As the pulse jerked in her throat, his hand went out, pressing his thumb against it, his eyes thoughtful.

'What are you doing?' She tried to retreat, but he slid an arm along the back of the couch to draw her to him.

'Just satisfying my curiosity,' he said softly.

When he smiled she thought of a tiger considering whether to eat now or later. When her tongue crept out to moisten suddenly dry lips, it was obvious he was tempted to satisfy his appetite right away.

His hand came up to cup the back of her head and with his other he pulled her swiftly towards him. For a fleeting moment he studied her face and she felt the pounding of her heart in her otherwise paralysed body. His mouth didn't find hers softly, as it had done in the past, it assaulted with a bruising desire to hurt, creating havoc wherever it explored.

Jane moaned as his kiss caught her off balance so that she was unable to control the passionate response which rendered her helpless. She tried but seemed incapable of protecting herself.

Paul drew her closer until she was welded to the shape of his lean body. As though the unsteadiness of her breathing inflamed him, his own breath rasped from his chest. His fingers slid between them, caressing her breasts before slipping through the low front of her dress.

'No!' She forced a strangled protest from tortured lungs, despairing that it was scarcely audible.

'Kiss me,' he ordered thickly, covering her mouth again.

The kiss went on and on and she felt herself start to weaken. Her blood rushed hotly through her veins and her mind blanked out to everything but the smell and taste of him, the pleasure he was arousing. Her lips were moist and parted. Hungrily she let him do as he liked with her, only flinching when the electricity generating between them began to sting. Vaguely she became aware that she was at the mercy of feelings too powerful to bear and for someone with her limited experience to cope with. It was like floodgates opening, releasing great torrents of sensation. Her fingers curled and flexed by her sides as she fought the desire to let them creep round his neck. As he crushed her to him, hurting yet threatening to drive her insane, she moaned weakly.

Overwhelmed, Jane let the world drift, fast losing all consciousness of it. It wasn't until Paul's hand pushed up her skirt and found the silken curves of her limbs that she really took fright and pulled away from him.

'What do you think you're doing?' she cried, trembling convulsively.

His face tightened over hard bones while his eyes darkened. 'Proving something,' he replied curtly.

'What, in heaven's name?' she gulped.

'That, though you might not have been married, you're no innocent little girl.'

'Innocent?' Wide-eyed she stared at him, hating the derision in his voice and what it seemed to imply. She had thought he had been trying to prove his power over her, but this was something else again.

'You've been around, haven't you?' he retorted grimly. 'You've probably slept with men for years. No girl responds the way you do without a lot of experience.'

Her glance attempted to slay him, so burning was her anger. 'You're completely wrong, but I'm not going to argue. I'm only thankful all men don't think the way you do!'

'You mean they don't all have my powers of discernment?'

'No!' she almost screamed at him through the hurt and fury building up inside her. 'I'm talking about your ability to jump to the wrong conclusions.'

His hard, sardonic eyes taunted her indignation with dry disrespect. 'I'm no boy to be easily fooled, you know. I could feel how you were going almost mad when I held you. What puzzles me is why you're trying to hide it.'

Jane gasped, wishing she could kill him on the spot, hating the way he merely laughed when her sparking eyes betrayed her. 'I'm not trying to hide anything, because I've nothing to hide!'

'I'm afraid,' Paul said quite coolly, 'I don't believe you.'

'Because you never wanted to, did you?' she cried. 'Since the beginning you've only wanted to believe the worst of me. Now you've doing your best to make me seem cheap!'

He smiled unpleasantly. 'Hardly cheap, my dear. I imagine if a man wants to sleep with you he has to be willing to pay heavily for the privilege.'

'Well, it won't ever be you!' she was incensed to retort. 'I'd rather die first!'

Paul gave a harsh crack of laughter. 'We might almost, at that. When we're together it certainly feels like an earthquake. I can think of worse fates than to die in your arms, my little Delilah!'

Colour surging to her cheeks, Jane sprang to her feet. 'Will you stop insulting me and just go!'

'As soon as we get one more thing straight, Paul agreed, getting up himself but in a more leisurely fashion. Taking her by the shoulders, his glance glittered menacingly on her flushed, angry face. 'You're beautiful and sexy, but while you're working on the Frey account, if you want an affair with a man, then it's going to be me. Try and make love with someone else and you might soon wish you'd never been born!'

Jane had to find Mark, the next day, to tell him she couldn't go on. She might have signed a contract, but even if it meant a prison sentence, she couldn't continue working for his firm. Other girls might be willing to sleep with the managing director or chairman, or whatever, in order to achieve their ambitions, but she had no such intentions. For one thing, she had never wanted this job in the first place. For another, she hated Paul Denyer and had no desire to have anything more to do with him. She doubted, if it ever came to it, that he would be serious about carrying out his despicable threats, but she had no wish to spend the next six months in a state of suspense and apprehension.

Bitterly she went over the short years of her life, as she travelled reluctantly to work. It was raining and the tube was crowded, the crush of wet bodies and sober faces doing nothing to discourage her unhappy thoughts. As a young girl, she had never been very confident, but she had managed, somehow, to cling to what other girls had often called her old-fashioned principles. She had shared a room with two other girls and managed to be content with what many would consider a rather dull lot. It just depended on what one wanted, she supposed.

Then had come the plane crash, after which she had been flung into an entirely different world, one which, strangely enough, she had come to accept and enjoy. From this, despite the trauma of a second upheaval, she

had emerged triumphantly to a future promising
security and even fame. Yet she found the whole thing
bewildering. There was no sense of co-ordination. She
had recovered her memory, but she still had no clear
idea of who she was or where she was going. And Paul
Denyer, whom during the terrible period of her amnesia
she had never hesitated to consult, had turned into a
brutal stranger whom she could neither like nor trust.

She had a photographic session that morning, but
had arrived early, hoping to see Mark. She had
considered ringing him at his apartment until she
realised she didn't know his number. It had been
raining when she left, when she got to the West End it
was still pouring down, making her glad she was
wearing her mac. It wasn't waterproof, though, and
before she reached International she was soaked.

There were few people about. Most of the staff didn't
start until nine-thirty and such weather didn't exactly
encourage them to get here sooner. Jane had the lift to
herself and slipped to the top floor unnoticed. To her
relief she saw Mark's figure reflected through the glass
of his office door, and with a quick knock she walked
in.

'Mark . . .' she began, then stopped abruptly. It
wasn't Mark but Paul. Wishing she could have sunk
through the floor, she stammered, 'I'm sorry, Mr
Denyer. I thought it was your—your brother.'

Paul regarded her bedraggled condition coolly. 'He
won't be in today, I'm afraid. Do you want to leave a
message?'

Jane was amazed that he could be so composed after
the scene of the night before. She was trembling and
would have given a year's salary to see him, just for
once, lose his cool! 'No, thank you,' she said stiffly. 'It
wasn't important.'

'For future reference, Miss Carey,' he said curtly,
'Mark doesn't have time to bother with anything that's
not urgent when he's supposed to be working.'

Prig! she thought angrily.

Paul ignored her obvious opinion of him as if it was of no account. 'Are you as wet underneath as you are on top?' he asked.

'I'm not sure——' she began uncertainly.

In a second he was beside her, removing her mackintosh. 'We've got quite a bit of money sunk in you,' he snapped impatiently as she tried to ward him off. 'It would be inconvenient, to say the least, if you went down with pneumonia!'

Flinging her coat aside, he touched the wet patches on her blouse, unbuttoning it swiftly as she struggled. Horrified, as she realised what he was doing, Jane again tried to stop him, but he merely pushed her protesting hands out of the way. Leaving her standing in her skirt and bra, he placed her wet clothes over a radiator.

'They should dry in a moment,' he said, coming back to her.

Quickly Jane wrapped her arms around herself. 'You have a nerve!' she exclaimed, her face scarlet.

'Among my other assets,' Paul agreed laconically, his eyes running over her.

'And you can stop looking!' she said fiercely.

'Just inspecting the collateral,' he replied lightly. 'You must agree I have a vested interest.'

She swallowed as he slid a hand over her bare shoulders, ready to scream if it went lower. 'You don't need to be so thorough!' she snapped.

'Maybe not,' he mocked, obviously intent on infuriating her further by bending his dark head to kiss her mouth.

When his arms slid to her hips, bringing her very close to him, she knew she would have screamed if his mouth hadn't stopped her. Seconds later, with his hardness almost hurting her, when he muttered against her lips, 'See what you do to me,' she found herself incapable of saying a word.

Then, as swiftly as he had taken hold of her, he put

her from him. 'There's plenty of hot coffee. You'd better have some.'

Five minutes later, having swallowed a hot drink and donned her now dry blouse, Jane made her way to the studios. For the first time she felt frightened more of herself than of Paul. When he held her she responded, like tinder to a flame. He made her feel wanton until she was ready to give herself to him, while she knew he was merely provoking her in order to punish her for crimes he believed she had committed and not yet atoned for. Her face pale, Jane shuddered, even more convinced that she must find a way of rescinding her contract before her whole world shattered in a thousand pieces and something happened from which she might never recover.

Paul hadn't said where Mark was and had ruthlessly diverted her, she suspected, before she could ask. She had a vague notion of quizzing the studio staff, but was kept so busy she never got the opportunity. Mrs Frey arrived, determined to be very sure she was getting exactly what she wanted. Before the contracts had been signed she had inspected a portfolio of photographs Jane had of herself and had a few preliminary shots taken, but there had been nothing like the rigorous session which took place today. Long before it was time to break for lunch Jane was exhausted, but as Mrs Frey's energy never flagged she felt almost ashamed of herself.

She had lunch with Keith Lester, the creative director, whose reputation depended on producing a sustained succession of brilliant and original advertising campaigns. He was older than Jane, but his mercurial personality made him appear younger than his years.

'If you've not already been snapped up,' he grinned, 'how about eating with me? We're going to be working together a lot and it will make everything so much easier if we get to know each other.'

'Do you have to ask all your models out?' she asked demurely.

His grin widened. 'Only those who look like you,' he confessed, to Jane's amusement.

They used a lot of TV stars who Jane believed looked even better, but she was intelligent enough to realise that Keith's invitation hadn't come entirely from the kindness of his heart. This morning she had been on edge, far from relaxed. Ben Dufton, one of the photographers, a young man with exceptional creative ability and bursting with originality, hadn't been too impressed, although he had done his best to hide her lack of experience from Olive Frey's eagle eye. What Keith intended to do was try and get her to lose some of her tenseness. He would talk to her, make her laugh and in general try and persuade her not to take this new assignment too seriously.

This was exactly what he did, and if the afternoon which followed proved as exhausting as the morning, at least Jane felt she was beginning to swim with the tide and not against it. Olive Frey must have been convinced of it, for she left at three with a satisfied smile on her face. At four the studio staff decided to call it a day, and despite her new confidence, Jane reached thankfully for her coat. She was walking quickly towards the lift when a secretary caught her, saying that Mr Denyer would like to see her before she went.

'Whereabouts?' Jane asked, feeling far from pleased and not a little apprehensive. Paul's attitude made his opinion of her very plain. She didn't believe he could have anything pleasant to say to her.

He hadn't, but being half prepared was a help. It enabled Jane to listen without outwardly flinching as he attacked her. He was sitting behind the desk which she had thought was Mark's, and didn't bother to rise as his secretary ushered her in and closed the door behind her. Nor did he ask her to sit down.

His silvery eyes went over her, dryly noting the

tiredness she didn't bother to hide. 'Finding the going too hard, Miss Carey?'

'Not altogether,' she replied coldly. 'I haven't had an assignment like this before, but I'm getting used to it.'

'Any new experience can prove exhausting,' he agreed suavely. 'Perhaps I'd be wiser to let you take it one at a time.'

What on earth was he on about now? And why were her cheeks growing hot when she had absolutely no idea? 'You wished to see me, Mr Denyer,' she said pointedly, inserting more ice in her voice.

'Ah, yes,' he nodded, his absent tones giving no warning of the bombshell he was about to drop. 'My mother's been on the phone.'

'Oh, how is she?' Jane exclaimed, her whole face lighting up.

Paul's hard mouth twisted. 'I imagine you found Coombe Park a lot more comfortable than where you are now.'

'Who wouldn't?' Jane saw no sense in lying about it. 'And your mother was very kind.'

'My mother,' he said curtly, 'is a very nice person, but she is also extremely impulsive and inclined to be foolish.'

Jane's head came up. 'I don't believe she's ever foolish, and if she does sometimes act without thinking, isn't that better than being like you?'

'I presume your remark's not meant to be flattering,' Paul retorted coolly, 'but I didn't bring you here to discuss my character. I take heart that it can't be worse than your own.'

'If we're swopping insults——' Jane began.

'No, we're not,' he cut in abruptly. 'I simply wanted to tell you to keep away from Coombe Park. My mother is itching to issue an invitation, and if you accept, knowing her, she wouldn't stop until either Mark or I felt obliged to marry you.'

'M-marry you!'

His grey eyes pierced her coldly. 'You don't have to look so innocently incredulous, my dear. For some inexplicable reason she likes you, and I don't doubt she could rely on your co-operation. Possibly you would bargain together—one of her sons in exchange for a couple of grandchildren in a corresponding number of years.'

Jane stared at him, not surprised to hear she looked incredulous. That was how she felt! 'You don't expect me to believe you would marry a girl just because your mother asked you to?' she breathed.

'There's Mark.'

So—now she realised. He wasn't thinking of himself. It was his brother who he considered might be vulnerable, and he didn't want him put at risk. Furiously, Jane gasped, 'Your opinion, of both your mother and myself, is nothing less than insulting! I don't know what it's based on . . .'

'My knowledge of women,' he snapped.

'I shouldn't think you know the first thing!' she spat, incensed, 'apart from your experiences in bed!'

'We're getting away from the subject,' he cut back, eyes glittering. 'I've already promised we'll go to bed together some time, but when I make love to you, my darling, you won't be wearing my wedding ring.'

As Jane glared at him speechlessly, his face darkened with derision. 'I want your promise,' he said.

'Promise?' she choked, every inch of her burning. 'Would you expect me to promise you anything after all that? You must be joking!'

Suddenly he was beside her, his hands holding her wrists, his glance searing into her. 'I'll have your assurance that you won't go near Coombe Park, and I don't care how long I have to wait for it.'

Shocked, Jane sagged, unable to even wipe the tears from her eyes as he imprisoned her hands. 'You leave me cold,' she whispered hoarsely.

Instantly his mouth came down, crushing hers

cruelly. He held her until she began trembling and the heat in her veins transmitted to her skin.

'Cold?' he mocked, raising his head.

'And disgusted!' she breathed, finishing her former sentence.

His jaw tight, his mouth a thin line, contemptuously he flung her away. 'If you won't promise, you leave me no alternative but to threaten. Go near Coombe Park and you'll rue the day, and never say I didn't warn you!'

Jane still felt shaken when she reached home and her landlady told her someone had left a message for her.

'A lady called, she wants you to ring back as soon as you can. I took her number.'

As Mrs Banks pointed to the telephone pad, Jane was startled to realise it was the number of Coombe Park she was gazing at. She had thought it might be Beth, from Scotland. Beth had been incredulous to hear that Jane was still alive and had promised to pay her a visit as soon as she could.

Half frozen with shock, Jane thanked Mrs Banks jerkily. 'I'll just take my things upstairs first.'

That was merely an excuse. There was nothing to stop her from ringing Mary Denyer immediately, but somehow she couldn't find the courage. In her lounge, Jane flung herself down in a chair feeling deathly weary. Since leaving Paul she hadn't allowed herself to think because, she admitted, she hadn't wanted to. She had decided not to worry over something which might not happen. She was sure Paul wouldn't only have talked to her. He would have discussed the situation with his mother, advising her to forget about Jane Carey and not to get in touch with her.

That Mrs Denyer had, made Jane very anxious. She didn't take what Paul had said about his mother wanting to see her married to one of her sons altogether seriously, but she saw no point in involving herself with Coombe Park again if it was going to cause controversy in the family. If she did long to renew her acquaintance with Mary and John Denyer, it must be because she scarcely remembered her own parents, and somehow, while she had stayed with them, they had seemed completely compatible. She missed them and they might miss her, but she feared she must refuse any invitation to visit them. Of course, she argued with herself, no one had actually issued an invitation yet. Perhaps Mary just wanted to ask how she was.

Knowing she couldn't put it off indefinitely, Jane ran back downstairs and picked up the phone. 'Mrs Denyer? It's Jane.'

'Oh, my dear!' Mary Denyer's sigh of relief was heartfelt. Jane wasn't surprised to catch the sound of tears in her voice. 'I'm so glad of an opportunity to speak to you,' Mary choked. 'These past few weeks have been dreadful!'

'I know,' Jane said huskily. 'I'm sorry.'

'Oh, my dear!' Mary reiterated, clearly striving for composure. 'Mark gave us your number but not your address, and it's difficult to talk over the phone. Would you come to dinner? Someone could pick you up within the next hour.'

'This evening!'

'Yes.'

Paul's name flashed in red letters before Jane's eyes. 'I'm afraid I can't, Mrs Denyer.'

'Oh, you have another engagement. Tomorrow, then?'

While searching frantically for another excuse, Jane suddenly decided Paul could go to the devil. Why should she allow herself to be threatened and browbeaten by a man who didn't give a damn for her? Swept by a feeling of complete recklessness, she was quickly impatient of her own caution.

Yet she couldn't altogether dispose of it. 'Will Paul be there?' she asked nervously.

'No, dear,' Mary replied, her tone so light that Jane

couldn't guess if she sensed her agitation. 'We don't see much of him you know, but tomorrow night I believe he has a business dinner. It was just something he mentioned to his father. He encourages John to believe his interest in the firm is still important. Of course we both know it isn't, but John appreciates it when Paul discusses things with him . . .'

Jane let her ramble on. Mary sounded slightly distracted and usually she was so precise. She had, though, been through a terrible time, and Jane began feeling very concerned for her. Mary would never lose control completely, she just wasn't that kind of person, but that didn't mean she wasn't as much in need of sympathy and help as anyone. And if she wanted to give it as well—well, what right had Paul to try and stop her?

Suddenly Jane felt it would be less than humane to refuse to go to Coombe Park. Paul had probably been bluffing, anyway, and it must be ludicrous to allow herself to be frightened by his idle threats. When Mary paused she said gently, 'I'll see you tomorrow evening, then. Will around seven be all right?'

She drew a tremulous breath when Mary replied happily, 'Oh, yes, dear, that will be lovely. We'll look forward to seeing you.'

CHAPTER SEVEN

THE following afternoon, just as Jane had managed to persuade herself that as Paul would be tied up with business affairs that evening, she had nothing to fear, he threw her back into a state of worry and confusion by inviting her out to dinner.

He was in the studio, and before he left he asked to see her in his office. 'I have a table booked for eight,' he said abruptly, when she arrived. 'I want to talk to you. I'll pick you up at seven-thirty.'

Jane's eyes widened and she went pale with fright as he obviously expected her to agree. Either his mother had made a mistake or his business engagement had been cancelled, but regardless as to what had happened, Jane realised she was in an awkward position.

'Couldn't we talk here?' she asked uneasily.

'No, Miss Carey.'

Jane bit her lip, wondering where her wits were. Even if she hadn't arranged to dine at Coombe Park, the way things were between Paul and herself wouldn't make for a very enjoyable evening! She could envisage them staring icily at each other over the entrée, exchanging heated words during the main course, and probably coming to blows over the sweet! A hysterical giggle rose in her throat and she choked.

'Are you trying to say something, Jane?'

She became conscious of Paul's darkening face as he waited impatiently for her to speak. Wildly she sought for an excuse.

'I can't think that you can have anything further to discuss with me. And anyway, I have a terrible headache.'

'Aspirin's very good.'

113

His voice was so dry, she realised he suspected her of lying and looked away from his narrowed eyes. 'I intend taking some when I get home,' she muttered.

Silkily he observed the guilty flush on her cheeks. 'It will be worse by then if you don't take something now.' He put out a hand to buzz for his secretary.

'No, please!' Jane's sharp cry stopped him. 'I'll be quite all right, if I have an early night.'

'In other words, you don't want to go out with me?'

'Not really.'

'Then why not say so,' he snapped, 'instead of inventing excuses?'

Jane's head was actually beginning to throb because of the tension between them. 'I don't really feel so good,' she said unhappily. 'And what would be the sense of spending a whole evening together when neither of us would enjoy it?'

'Speak for yourself, Miss Carey,' he retorted.

Because she didn't understand him, she was driven to reply tartly in her own defence. 'You're always trying to get at me. You can't expect such a prospect to fill me with joy!'

'Perhaps not,' Paul startled her by sighing moodily as his eyes raked her strained features.

Her blue eyes were feverishly bright while her lower lip visibly trembled. Hunger flooded over her, making her recklessly regret refusing to go out with him. 'Paul——' she began huskily.

'Run along.' He didn't seem to hear as he dismissed her curtly. 'Go on!' he said more harshly, as she frowned and hesitated, 'before I change my mind. I'll find another girl who enjoys my company better.'

Jane was suddenly aghast and wasn't quick enough to hide it. As foolish tears sprang to her eyes, he immediately saw them. 'So you don't like the idea of another girl?' he murmured, closing in on her, his taunting glance dropping to her unsteady mouth, his hands on ther shoulders. 'Now I wonder why?'

Shaken, Jane wrenched away from him, before his lips carried out what his eyes threatened, and her traitorous body could start clinging to his. Even to be near him reduced her to the level of a mindless idiot, and she hated to remember what his kisses could do!

'Goodnight!' she choked, rushing from the office while her legs still had the strength to carry her, not daring to look back to see his derisive glance following her, full of the knowledge that, despite all her protests, he still had a devastating power over her.

Paul didn't discover she was visiting Coombe Park until the following week. When she was there the second time and he arrived unexpectedly, looking coldly furious to see her, she wished apprehensively that she had had the sense to stay away.

Her first visit had gone well, but naturally, because of what had happened, it had been a rather sad occasion. Jane had been relieved to find that Mark had relayed to his parents much of what she had told him, but even the discussing of small points still to be cleared up had proved a strain and brought a certain heaviness to the atmosphere.

Jane hadn't expected it to be otherwise, and had been glad of the chance to express her sympathy personally and to apologise for leaving Coombe Park so abruptly after her memory returned.

Mary completely understood, and as Jane left she had begged her to come again. 'You've been a great help, dear,' she said gently. 'It was a shock to learn that you had never been Colin's wife, especially as we'd grown so fond of you, but now that we've found you again, both John and I hope you'll come and see us as often as you can.'

Nothing would have pleased Jane better, but while she didn't try and hide the affection she felt for Coombe Park and its occupants, she hesitated. 'Paul doesn't know I'm here,' she had confessed unhappily, and recalling how he had looked a few hours ago in his office, she shuddered to think what he might do if he found out.

Mary had glanced at her shrewdly but merely said lightly, 'Paul doesn't have to know everything.'

'But he might not approve if I come again,' Jane had said nervously.

'Leave him to me,' Mary had smiled, going on to name a future date to which Jane had felt forced to agree.

Because Paul didn't mention her visit to Coombe Park, she allowed herself to be lulled into a false sense of security. Just how false, she was soon to realise.

During working hours she saw quite a lot of Paul. He was frequently in the studio watching her progress with the photographers. Jane often wished he would stay away, for every time he was there, with his eyes steady upon her, a ridiculous feeling of guilt would sweep through her as she thought of her visit to his parents and another one arranged. She didn't have to feel she was deceiving him, she argued silently. If he made rules he had no right to make, he should expect them to be broken.

But he was like a dark threat in the background, and even when she wasn't looking at him she could feel his eyes burning into her. It made a shiver run along her nerves at the sensation it produced, and her blood would begin to pound with a mixture of fear and excitement. Paul might have sensed she had something on her mind, because he often stared at her so intently she was sure he was trying to read it. It got to such a pitch that she was unable to relax, and one day she confessed as much to Keith Lester.

Keith had gone out of his way to get her to relax when she had first come, and he wondered why she had returned to her former stiffness.

'I don't find it easy to work when Mr Denyer's around,' Jane tried to sound as if she'd no idea why. 'Does he always have to see what's going on?'

'I shouldn't take any notice, if I were you,' Keith replied soothingly. 'He does appear to be taking an unusual interest in the Frey account—but then it's an important one.'

Jane didn't derive much comfort from this. 'I thought he spent most of his time abroad,' she said.

Keith shrugged. 'He'll probably be off again one of these days. Meanwhile, darling,' he grinned at Jane, pleading wryly, 'he is the boss and there's nothing much we can do about it. If he wants to hang around, you'll just have to pretend he's not there.'

Nodding unhappily, Jane didn't say she would find this advice difficult to follow. From what she gathered, from odd snatches of conversation she had overheard, Paul rarely showed his face during studio sessions, and she guessed he was doing so now, not so much because of the importance of the Frey account but deliberately to annoy her. As Keith pointed out, of course, there was little she could do about it, but she found it impossible to ignore him.

She dressed carefully for her next visit to Coombe Park, choosing a simple but stylish dress in her favourite shade of blue. Since starting to work on the Frey account she had had to submit to being groomed to perfection, and while she personally disliked the model girl image she now projected, she had to admit it was flattering. Now her pale brown hair had a wonderful gloss and moved beautifully every time she did, and her skin glowed with good health and the silky smoothness attained from the use of good cosmetics. She supposed she ought to appreciate looking so attractive, but she often thought of her old self with nostalgia. She felt she had been much happier struggling to the office through the morning rush hour when she was a typist than she had ever been since.

When she arrived at Coombe Park, to her delight she was met by the dogs before Mary appeared and banished them to the kitchens. When Jane confessed how much she missed them, Mary said she must come for a weekend and take them out.

'It gets dark too early in the evenings,' she smiled. 'There wouldn't be time after you finish work.'

'The exercise would do me good,' Jane laughed, without committing herself, smiling at James as he took her coat and fussed around her as though she was a prodigal daughter come home again.

After dinner they returned to the drawing-room and for a while talked about her work. John Denyer laughed when Jane confessed she wasn't over-fond of modelling and would rather be a secretary.

'One of these days,' he teased, 'you'll meet the right man and get married, which will solve your problem for you! You can then devote the rest of your life to looking after your husband and family.'

This, as was to be expected, had Mary and Jane quickly accusing him of being old-fashioned. Secretly, Jane knew there was nothing she would like better than to have a family and home of her own, but somehow, perhaps because she felt so deeply about it, she was reluctant to say so. Mary, although she hadn't worked since she had married, had surprisingly modern views on the subject and the ensuing discussion was lively, if no one took it altogether seriously.

It was in the middle of this, and just after James had served coffee, that Paul walked in. Jane felt her hands shake and she hastily put down her coffee cup before she dropped it. It was obvious that both Mary and John were as surprised as she was to see him, but she also felt frightened. Last week, when he had asked her to go out with him, she hadn't told him she was coming here, and when he hadn't renewed his invitation she had decided whatever it had been that he had wanted to discuss hadn't been important. Now, with his eyes blazing accusations of deceit, his disapproval, as it had been able to since she had first known him, made her miserable. It was no use telling herself scornfully to tilt her chin and return Paul's icy stare. She was ready to sink through the floor!

'It's not often we see you at this time of night,' Mary spoke briskly to her formidable son after a swift glance at Jane's white face. 'Were you just passing? Would you like something to drink?'

'I'll have some coffee,' he replied, without answering her first query. Sitting down beside Jane, he acknowledged her presence coldly. 'Good evening, Miss Carey.'

Jane flushed as she noticed his father's brows draw together. 'Good evening,' she returned stiffly.

His eyes slid over her, slowly and deliberately. 'You didn't mention you were revisiting old haunts. I presume this is the first time?'

Jane smiled woodenly, hoping he would take this for granted. 'Your parents asked me,' she said hoarsely.

'Why didn't you say so?' he attacked more directly.

Jane closed her eyes, aware that to Mary and John they probably sounded as if they were having a normal conversation. It was no good protesting she hadn't seen him, he had been in and out of the studio all day!

'I must have forgotten,' she murmured lamely. 'When I'm working I rarely think of anything else.'

'Is that a fact?' he drawled hatefully, thanking Mary for his coffee but ignoring her puzzled attempts to intervene.

'Yes.' Jane's already pink cheeks went scarlet, then paled. She knew, they both knew, this wasn't true. Every time Paul came to watch her working and their eyes met, she was sure he was deviously aware that for her the rest of the world faded. Maybe he put it down to many things, including fear. She breathed a half desperate sigh of relief that he couldn't read the secrets of her heart, but that was little consolation when she realised the plight she was in. Once he had her alone he was going to demand some straight answers, and she shuddered to think what that might mean.

'Have you had dinner, Paul?' Mary asked, with unusual determination. 'James could easily get you something.'

'I've had something,' he thanked her briefly. 'I called to see how you were, not for what I could get.'

Jane had never heard him speaking so curtly to his mother, although he wasn't always patient with her. Instinctively she guessed his last remark had been aimed at herself. Did he really believe she was out for all she could get? She shivered as she met eyes narrowed contemptuously and saw them deepen with suspicion as his father remarked happily,

'Your mother and I have spent a lovely evening with Jane. We're trying to persuade her to come for a weekend.'

'Would I be invited too?' Paul asked sardonically.

'You know you can come any time,' Mary retorted, frowning.

'Then we'll come together,' he replied suavely, smiling almost tigerishly, his hard mouth twisting with mocking amusement, his silvery glance never wavering from Jane's dismayed face. 'We'll let you know.'

Bitterness flooded to the back of Jane's throat, bringing a red mist before her eyes. Realising with horror how he was manipulating her helplessness to suit his own ends, she knew if they had been alone she would have tried to hit him. She was horrified at the fierceness of the emotion she felt and despairing of her inability to express it.

Her face was still for a second as she stared at him. Now his expression was masked, his eyes unreadable as he threw the ball into her court and waited. Something was boiling inside her head, the residue of defeat because of her inability to sever herself from him completely. Much as she might refuse to admit it, that part of her life after the plane crash, until the day she left here, was the only part which had any reality. All that time she had clung to Paul until unconsciously she must have formed a bond almost impossible to break.

When she remained silent, Mary said eagerly, 'Why not make it this weekend, before you change your minds?'

Paul shrugged lightly and said, 'Why not?' while Jane was still floundering. Then, to her further dismay, she heard Mary, evidently encouraged by this, suggesting something else.

'I don't like the idea of Jane living where she does, especially as there's so much room at Coombe Park. She could quite easily live here and commute every day. Couldn't she, Paul?' she appealed to her son.

'Would you like that, Jane?'

Jane swallowed to hear her name on Paul's lips after so long. It was like being given a drink after being parched. She had a crazy desire to ask him to say it again.

'I think I'd better stay where I am for the moment,' she replied slowly, making an effort to show how much she appreciated Mary's kindness by smiling at her gratefully.

'Of course, dear,' Mary agreed, clearly believing Jane would eventually give in.

Before anything more might be suggested, Jane rose quickly to her feet. 'I really must be going!' she exclaimed, pretending to be shocked at the time.

'Good heavens, it's actually nine-thirty!' Paul mocked, beside her in a flash. 'I'll run you back.'

'I shouldn't dream of putting you out,' she retorted, wondering hollowly if she hadn't fallen into a trap of her own making. She had considered the possibility of Paul making such an offer for the past few minutes, but had decided that as he had only just arrived he wouldn't be leaving until later. At all costs she had wanted to avoid being alone with him, and it frustrated her to find how easily she had been thwarted.

'I'm sure you wouldn't want to drag James out on

such an evening,' Paul said with emphasis. 'The fog was bad enough when I came in. I shudder to think what it's like now!'

Jane hadn't actually believed in the fog until they were on their way. Paul's car was parked directly in front of the house and she thought it was darkness swirling about it, rather than fog. Sinking in her seat, she found it impossible to be over-concerned about the weather. She was feeling very young and uncertain, confused by her own emotions to the point of scarcely daring to speak for fear of saying something she might regret.

Because she had her eyes closed she didn't immediately realise that the car's headlights barely penetrated the murky blackness through which they were travelling. When something warned her of possible danger and her eyes flew open, she gasped with alarm.

'Paul,' she turned to him, cold with apprehension, 'can you see to drive? Shouldn't you park somewhere and wait till this clears?'

'Just sit back and keep quiet,' he replied tersely. 'You've caused enough trouble for one night.'

'Trouble?' she whispered indignantly. 'What do you mean by trouble? I didn't ask you to take me home. I had no idea you would turn up as you did!'

'Neither of us should have been here,' he retorted between his teeth, 'Neither of us would have been if you'd used your common sense.'

His meaning being all too explicit, Jane flushed. 'Who told you where I was?'

'No one.' He flicked the wipers into action then off again impatiently. 'You looked so guilty today it made me begin to think. You weren't going out with another man, I was pretty sure of that, so there could only be one other thing. And this isn't the first time, is it?' he added savagely.

'No,' she confessed unhappily.

'The evening I asked you to have dinner with me,' he continued relentlessly, 'the convenient headache.'

'I'm sorry,' she sighed helplessly, 'but don't you see? I couldn't tell you when you'd forbidden me to go, and how could I say no to your mother?'

'The same way as you say no to me,' he jeered, changing gear and pulling up sharply.

There was another car barely a yard in front of them, its rear fog-light barely visible. 'Great, isn't it?' Paul muttered sardonically, as Jane drew a frightened breath. 'We'll be lucky if we're home by midnight.'

It wasn't midnight, but it took an hour longer than it would normally have done before they reached the West End. The fog hadn't lifted, it was still dense, and when Paul stopped with a sigh of relief, Jane strained to try and see where they were.

'Outside my apartment,' he told her curtly, when she had to ask.

'Your apartment?' she blinked in bewilderment. 'Are you just calling in?'

'No, I'm staying.' He turned a slightly haggard face towards her, his eyes showing definite signs of strain.

Jane said anxiously, 'But you promised to take me home.'

'I'm not doing ten more miles in this!' he retorted. 'Not for anybody!'

Jane was blind to the white lines about his mouth, being too concerned over her own position. 'I'll have to get a taxi, then!'

'Not a hope,' he snapped, clearly with growing impatience. 'You may be beautiful, my darling, but it usually takes more than a pretty face to persuade a man to commit suicide. You have no other option but to stay with me.'

'With—you?'

'Don't worry,' he met her apprehensive eyes sarcastically, 'much as I'd like to make love to you, I don't think I'd be capable of even holding your hand, let alone seducing you. If that term's appropriate for a girl who's undoubtedly been seduced many times before!'

Jane knew a flash of sheer rage, the feeling exploding through her body as Paul indifferently expressed his insolent opinion of her. She restrained an angry outburst with difficulty, deciding painfully that what he thought of her didn't matter, and that it might annoy him more if she showed dignity rather than anger. 'I'll stay,' she said coolly, 'if you'll promise not to touch me.'

'Haven't I already said so?' He ran a long-fingered hand wearily through his dark hair. 'You can go to bed straight away, if you like, and there's a lock on your bedroom door.'

His obvious tiredness, his assurances, locks on her door. Why did she feel it wasn't enough? Yet what else could she do but go with him? It had been a terrible drive through the fog. Few but a remarkably expert driver might have made it. It would be unreasonable to ask anyone to go any farther when it wasn't absolutely imperative, and if they crashed into another car, other lives could be put at risk as well as their own.

'Very well,' she gave in reluctantly, forcing the words past the tightness in her throat.

Mrs Denyer had once told her that Paul kept no staff in his apartment, preferring to use the catering facilities available and retain his privacy. A vague hope that he might have altered this arrangement died at the complete silence which met them as they shot up in the lift and entered his flat.

'What about my landlady?' Jane remembered her suddenly, unable to think why she hadn't done so before. 'She'll be worried about me.'

Paul glanced at her enigmatically as she stood shivering, pulling her velvet cloak tighter around her although the central heating was on and the apartment was warm.

'You can ring her in the morning, before I take you to work, and explain how you couldn't get home in the fog. She won't be waiting up for you, will she? You have your own key.'

He knew she had it, because he had seen it when he had been there, there was no sense in denying it. Glumly Jane nodded.

'Can I go to bed——'

Derisively his lips quirked. 'Are you always in such a hurry?'

'I hate your hateful innuendoes!'

He contrived to look innocently hurt at the sight of her accusing face. 'I was merely about to suggest you might like a drink.'

'Then you can keep your suggestions to yourself! You promised I could go straight to bed. Where's my room?'

'My God!' he breathed. 'Proper little matriarch, aren't we? Women—may heaven protect me from them!'

'I don't notice you struggling very hard!' she snapped, unable to forget a recent newspaper shot of him dining with a dazzling blonde.

'I said protect, not isolate,' he drawled.

God, he must be shameless! 'My—room?' Jane choked angrily.

'Please yourself,' he shrugged dismissively. 'Second on the right along the corridor. But remember,' he taunted, 'in your haste to get to sleep, it will only bring the morning sooner, and tomorrow is to be a day of reckoning.'

Knowing what he was warning her of sent Jane into a panic. As she went into the bedroom and closed the door she felt her hands trembling. Paul had thrown one or two cutting remarks about her going to Coombe Park, but she guessed, because of the fog, he had barely got started. She had heard hints at work that his temper could be formidable and she had no wish to feel the full force of it descending on her head. It was to be hoped that after a good night's sleep he would change his mind over tackling her about Coombe Park and feel able to forgive her.

She breathed a sigh of relief on discovering she had her own bathroom, as it saved her from having to search outside and probably running into Paul again. But while this solved one problem, she was still left with another. She had nothing to sleep in. After opening one or two drawers and finding them empty, she decided to sleep in her pants and bra, which was all she was wearing under her dress. It was warm enough. Apart from feeling naked, she should be quite all right.

The bed was comfortable, the sheets silky smooth against her skin. The room was quietly furnished with deep carpets and curtains of obviously the best quality and in toning colours. She was almost sorry to put out the light and hide it from sight. It was such a complete contrast from her own very basic bed-sitter.

She found it difficult to get to sleep, although she was so tired. Not even the warm shower she had taken helped her to relax. A certain feeling of guilt preyed on her mind as she realised she had been wrong in not telling Paul she was visiting his parents. Maybe he hadn't any right to order her not to, but she did owe him a lot—too much to go completely against his wishes. And if she had managed to find the courage to defy him, that same courage should have enabled her to be honest with him. Restlessly she tossed and turned, unable to escape her uneasy thoughts, unaware that she was fast reducing her bedclothes to an untidy heap.

When at last she did fall asleep, the turmoil she was experiencing must have brought back her old nightmares, for she woke with a strangled cry to find Paul shaking her, his face gleaming pale above her.

Dazed, her eyes widening with fright, she gazed at him. 'Paul?' she whispered.

'Before you ask what I'm doing here,' he said

bitingly, 'you should have heard yourself screaming. Fortunately you must have forgotten to lock the door, so I didn't have to break it down. Your old trouble, I suppose?'

'Yes,' there was a sob in her voice and she found herself clinging to him. 'Oh, please, Paul,' she moaned, 'just hold me!'

'I'm a man, not a saint,' he muttered dryly against the top of her head, as she all but threw herself at him.

'Please!' she begged again, entirely distraught.

'I'm doing my best,' he said roughly.

After a few minutes her terror subsided, enough to allow her to speak. 'I was on the plane . . .'

'It's maybe time you were,' he retorted, 'then perhaps you'd be able to lay a few ghosts!'

The very thought of flying alarmed her. 'Please don't even talk about it,' she pleaded, her voice muffled against his chest.

'You'd rather put up with bad dreams all your life?'

'I'm sure they'll go away eventually,' she said huskily. 'The doctors said they should.'

'People are optimists,' he shrugged. 'You shouldn't believe everything you're told. Not blindly, anyway. You have to help yourself.'

She felt the movement of his shoulder under her cheek. There might be something in what he was saying, but she didn't want to listen to his advice. Within the circle of his arms she felt safe and marvellously confident that nothing could touch her. She was already clinging to him, but as he stirred her arms tightened, refusing to let him go.

'You're all I need,' she breathed.

'The old antidote,' he muttered dryly. 'I'm quite willing to try it again and to hell with the consequences, but are you?'

If Jane had been conscious of anything outside their two selves, she might have hesitated, but her mind was confused and she was ready to take advantage of it. She felt frightened and lonely because of her dreams and hungry for the comfort only Paul seemed able to give.

Silently she nodded, her heart beginning to race as he held her closer and his hands began moving sensuously over her. When they touched her bare skin, reminding her searingly of how little she had on, the wanton feelings he aroused defeated all sense of caution.

As his lean fingers gently slid round her nape, to allow his thumbs to lift her face up to him, she found herself locked in a breathless, trancelike immobility. Her hair streamed over her shoulders, scenting the air with its delicate fragrance, and she felt him tremble as he breathed in deep into his lungs.

'Beautiful,' he muttered, his arms tightening, so that her breasts were crushed against the hardness of his chest. 'Kiss me,' he commanded softly, his mouth touching hers teasingly.

A surge of intense yearning swept over her, burning like an unquenchable flame, and with more ardour than expertise she pressed her lips to his. Then she became aware of his mocking amusement. Stung, she withdrew, realising he was laughing at her. 'Damn you!' she cried, choking on tears of humiliation.

'You scarcely know the first thing, do you?' he taunted. 'What about your previous lovers? Didn't they teach you anything, or were they only interested in their own satisfaction?'

Horrified by his derision as well as her own shameful subjection, Jane stiffened away from him, but he refused to let her escape.

'Only a minute ago,' he reminded her coldly, 'you were practically begging me to take you, so you can stop struggling and pretending you've changed you mind.'

His eyes darkened appreciably, all traces of humour had disappeared. Helplessly Jane stared at him, knowing she couldn't deny his accusations. And, as he held her ruthlessly, a wave of desire rose within her again, engulfing every other thought.

'Oh, Paul . . .' she sighed, as he began covering her face and neck in swift, searching kisses, 'I need you . . .'

'My needs have gone unsatisfied too long,' he retorted thickly, pushing her back on the bed and stretching alongside her. He turned his body half over hers and the impact was frightening. When he fused their lips the sensation of heat and fire had her squirming under him.

Jane was lost as the insistence of his mouth sent the blood scalding through her veins, and she whimpered as needles of sensation went shooting through her.

'What is it now?' he asked impatiently, raising his head.

'I'm frightened,' she whispered, quite truthfully.

'You always are,' he retorted cynically. 'You should be used to it. Those who live by their wits are usually aware of the risks they take and learn to accept their fears as part of their life-style.'

Whatever did he mean? Would he never learn to trust her? Obviously not, if the contempt glinting from his eyes was anything to go by. She must have been mad to have been about to give herself to a man who despised her so. For him it would be sex, nothing more or less.

Jane shivered, reading the look in the narrowed grey eyes which seemed to confirm her suspicions. 'You'd better go,' she began, trying to speak coolly.

'No.' Ignoring her strangled protests, Paul began caressing her breasts, threatening to send her spinning into oblivion. 'We've talked enough,' he snapped, finding the clip of her bra and flinging it off, leaving her completely naked. 'That's better,' he breathed harshly.

Immediately she tried to grab something to cover herself, but he grasped both her wrists in a cruel grip, holding them above her head while he eased himself up to survey her trembling body. 'I have the experience, you know,' he said thickly, 'to make this a very enjoyable occasion. In an hour's time I can guarantee you'll be begging me to take you again.'

Anger flared raggedly within her, but when she tried to meet his suddenly burning gaze, her own reactions defeated her. Helpless tears fell on her cheeks as she realised she wasn't ashamed of her feelings, as she had been a few moments ago. She felt she had been born to lie in his arms, a budding Eve who, with Paul for Adam, would never have been tempted to leave the Garden of Eden.

As he lowered himself on to her again and his lips found hers, the shock of intense pleasure she felt sent her arms curving feverishly round his neck. Her breasts swelled in the cup of his hands as one kiss melted into another, and a slow languor was relaxing her limbs, making her utterly pliant. With a groan, as her soft lips parted, he crushed them with the hunger of a starving man, and suddenly she was responding with a wildness she hadn't known she possessed.

'Help me off with this,' he muttered huskily, but managed to get rid of his robe while her fingers were still fumbling clumsily. As the beat of mutual desire throbbed between them, she gazed at his tall, strong body, fascinated by its male beauty, which she was seeing for the first time. He was magnificent, and the knowledge came inescapably that she wanted him— now!

When the bareness of their bodies came together, and his mouth and tongue teased each pink-tipped peak in turn, a white-hot heat started deep down inside her. A new ferocity came to his lovemaking and as his teeth closed on a taut nipple, a shock-wave went right through her. She gasped, her nails digging fiercely into his shoulders as she tried to tell him what he was doing to her.

'Steady,' he muttered thickly. 'I want every part of you, my darling, but we don't have to hurry.'

Jane breathed deeply against his chest as his expert

caresses brought a mounting intoxication. Feverishly she ran her hands over his back, delighting in the feel of strong muscles rippling under his smooth skin. He groaned, raising her body slightly, holding it against him, until she could feel her passion equalling his.

'Are you ready?' he whispered hoarsely, and she felt a shudder run right through him as she nodded blindly.

CHAPTER EIGHT

JANE felt her heart race faster when, as she replied, flames seemed to leap into his eyes, scorching her. With a smothered exclamation, he pressed her yearning body closer, guiding her hungrily groping hands.

'Touch me—here,' he groaned thickly, pushing them against the flatness of his stomach. She felt the hardness of his thighs and thought she might faint.

'Paul!' she breathed, actually hearing the unsteadiness of her own voice.

Her lips parted as he swooped on them, having already made himself drunk on the distended fullness of her nipples. She moaned deep in her throat at her first real experience of intense sexual excitement. He delved into the depth of her mouth, tasting her burning sweetness, devouring her as he pulled her completely beneath him, straining against her, making no attempt to hide his thrusting needs. Fire flowed along Jane's limbs as she lifted herself to meet him. She had no experience to help her, just the passion and love throbbing wildly within her and an instinctive desire to please.

Then suddenly it was over. Shock held her immobile as, without warning, Paul abruptly levered himself from her. Turning his back on her, he roughly brushed her arms aside as she attempted to hold him, taking no notice of her wounded cry. She felt the ache inside her begin to fade, but like a bleeding wound she was conscious of her body's disappointment.

Totally bewildered, she gazed at him. He sat on the edge of the bed, his face buried in his hands, as if he didn't want her to see what lay in it. Despite herself, she still felt a surge of desire as her eyes rested on the strong contours of his powerful figure.

Then, unexpectedly, he reared his head, turning it sharply to look at her, catching her expression of awareness.

'You wanton little bitch!' he ground out. 'You trade on sexuality, don't you? And I nearly fell for it again!'

'Paul!' she whispered, her face whitening. 'I don't understand you . . .'

'Possibly not,' he jeered coldly, 'but oh, lady, you're no mystery to me! You've the instincts of an alley cat and you know how to use them. I still don't believe you ever lost your memory. You knew you were on to a good thing when you first got on that plane in Italy. When you woke up in hospital and discovered what had happened, you must have imagined your luck was improving by the minute!'

'We—we've been through all this before,' she protested unsteadily, willing her pulse to slow down.

'You must recall being at school,' he snarled. 'Hell, it can't be that long since! There you were taught to say things over and over again until you learned them by heart. Well, you'd better get this in your head and make sure it stays there. I'm not for you, neither is Mark!'

'Mark?' Cold with despair, her voice trembled. 'I'm not sure what you're talking about, but I don't love Mark.'

'You don't love anybody,' Paul laughed, 'but yourself.'

'That's not true,' cried her heart. 'I love you!' but she stopped the words with fingers over her bruised mouth. If he even suspected she loved him it would place a weapon in his hands greater than the one he was flaying her with now. And her love was so new, strong but like a delicate flower which might shrivel in the frost of his contempt.

Her cheeks grew hot, her whole body in turmoil as she made discoveries which proved almost too much for her. 'You're mistaken about a lot of things.' Raising heavy lashes, she stared at him miserably.

'You're like creeping ivy,' he rasped, as though she had never spoken. 'You cling, choking. If all else fails you're determined to get back to Coombe Park.'

'I like your parents,' she said shakily.

'I imagine you're even fonder of a certain car garaged there. One you were promised when you obtained a driving licence!'

'Oh, Paul!' She felt so wounded she feared she might break down completely. Pain and anguish filled her that his opinion of her should be so degrading. She put out a tentative hand to touch him, but he knocked it aside.

'Oh, Paul!' he mimicked savagely. 'God, what do you think I am? I know what you are, fortunately. The evidence I collected reads like a second-rate novel!'

'How dare you?' she breathed, suddenly furious at the intrusion this suggested into her privacy. This time her anger jerked her towards him so her fingers succeeded in contacting his arm, her nails sharply penetrating the bare skin. It didn't strike her as incongruous that they were both sitting naked, talking to each other like enemies. All she wanted to do was hurt him.

'Are you trying to tear me apart?' he asked scornfully, again shaking her off with contempt. But he didn't move away. She felt his breath on her face as he stared at her, saw the dark red colour under his cheekbones as he snapped, 'You're a tease, aren't you? and I'm not the only one who thinks so. I talked to a man when I called at your old flat—name of Jack. He was uncouth but extremely enlightening.'

As Jane's eyes widened incredulously, he continued ruthlessly, 'There was also the photographer who went to Italy with you. You promise but don't deliver, he said.'

Cirero! Jane flushed. He had fancied her all right, but she had neither liked or encouraged him. She hadn't encouraged Jack Adams, either. He was Pat's boy-

friend and always had been. Both she and Beth had
hated the leering advances he had been fond of making
behind Pat's back. Revenge must have driven him to
tell Paul vindictive lies, but she couldn't forgive Paul for
listening to him.

'None of it's true!' she cried sharply.

'Oh, yes, it is, lady.' Staring derisively into her
feverish blue eyes, Paul shot a hand out to curve
roughly round her nape. 'But don't think you're going
to escape me!'

As she felt his fingers, under the heaviness of her
hair, caressing her neck, a sweet, pulsating hunger
flooded over her, so she had to grit her teeth to prevent
herself from responding.

'You can't want me, not after all you've accused me
of,' she whispered wildly.

'My mind doesn't,' he shrugged, 'but my body does.
Look at me.' Brutally he grasped her again as she
flinched back, making her gaze on the evidence he
didn't try to hide. 'So you see,' he snarled as her cheeks
blanched, then flushed hotly and the breath gasped
from her shaking mouth, 'exactly what you do to
me?'

His desire burnt her and she couldn't understand her
own blind reaction. She felt branded by his fire and
arrogance, yet it was her own total abandonment she
feared most. There was a furnace of desire inside her,
making fierce demands. It was a sensuality, a
wantonness she had never known she possessed, and
she didn't know what to do about it.

In a daze of bewildered panic, she spoke as much to
herself as to Paul. 'We have nothing in common . . .'

'What we have is enough,' with deliberate emphasis,
he touched her exquisite breasts. 'Physically we're
perfectly attuned. Every time I kiss you I can feel the
heat in your skin, your blood leaping to meet mine, but
I won't have you over an excuse.'

'An—excuse?'

There was no pity for her obvious confusion. 'Bad dreams, provocation, your pretence of needing help when it's something else you want. No, my darling,' he grated, his voice as hard as his eyes, 'I'm not going to be trapped into taking advantage of you that way. You're going to be begging at my feet, not pretending you're helpless and frightened, depending on my compassion to make things easy for you. You'll be crying for mercy before I'm finished with you, but you won't be getting any!'

Horrified, Jane watched as his teeth snapped and he rose from the bed. Pain blocked her throat as she followed his swift progress across the room and her ears seemed to ring to the slamming of the door. Instinctively she knew that if he hadn't left quickly he might have hit her, but there was no room beside the misery in her heart for feelings of relief. Whatever happened between them in the future, the only thing she could be assured of was his hate. With a sob she turned her face into her pillows and wept.

In the morning, Jane's eyes were puffy and red, and there were black rings around them. She had done her best with a shower, but while the cool water was reviving, it couldn't disguise the ravages to her face. Staring with dismay at her reflection, she felt she would have given anything for some make-up, but she had nothing with her.

Knowing she couldn't hide in her room for ever, she went to find Paul. He was in the kitchen, busy with the percolator. There was bacon sizzling under the grill and a pan with fried bread and eggs. Paul was superbly fit and apparently he let nothing interfere with his appetite. His mocking glance told her she wasn't going to, anyway!

With a shudder, she sat down, fearing that if she didn't her legs might collapse. She had thought she didn't feel so good when she got out of bed—now she knew she didn't!

'Good morning,' he said blandly. 'How many eggs would you like?'

She only managed to restrain a shudder, but at least he hadn't asked if she had slept well!

'I'll just have toast, if you don't mind.'

She tried not to glance at him after the first time. Again she wished she had had something to disguise her paleness, the bruises on her mouth. His astute gaze missed nothing. He noted the strain on her delicate features grimly as he served her with coffee.

'Toast's just coming up,' he said shortly.

'Thank you.' She wondered how they could be talking to each other so formally.

He helped himself to bacon and eggs, although he seemed to lose his appetite, too, as he sat down beside her. He was dressed for the office in a dark suit. There was a remoteness and coolness about him which she envied. Bitterly she wished he wasn't so handsome, that he hadn't the ability, no matter what the circumstances, to make her heart beat faster.

Apparently his cooking didn't please him this morning, for he concentrated on his coffee, not even bothering to share the toast. 'I've rung for a taxi. It will be here in ten minutes. Of course if you're not ready it can wait.'

'A taxi?' Jane had imagined she would be going to work with Paul and her glance flew stupidly to his.

For a moment, as their eyes met, his mouth tightened. 'It will take you home,' he explained shortly. 'You can get another after you've changed. You can't go to the studio like that.'

She was confused as to his motives. She realised she wasn't suitably dressed, but he could be trying to make things easier for her by covering her tracks. 'I understand,' she nodded dully, looking away from him.

He was watching her closely now, his eyes boring into

her, their impact making her head whirl. 'Jane,' he said sharply, 'look at me!'

Reluctantly she obeyed, not trying to hide her resentment.

'How long do you usually sulk?' he asked flatly.

'I'm not sulking.'

'Aren't you?'

She stared at him with bitter dislike, hating the new kind of intimacy lying between them. What had happened last night—through the night, couldn't, she was beginning to realise, be pushed aside and forgotten so easily. She wished it could.

'No,' her voice was low and angry, 'I'm merely regretting a lot of things. The fog, mainly. If it hadn't been for that I wouldn't have been here, but the fact that I am here doesn't give you the right to accuse me of sulking.'

'As well as everything else?'

He spoke with such a savage softness that she flushed. 'At least I've learned you don't trust me. My side of the story about Colin—you've never believed a word of it!'

His mouth twisted, the grey eyes icy. 'Would you have believed me, if our positions had been reversed?'

'I think so,' she replied unsteadily, but with a ring of conviction. 'If our positions had been reversed, I wouldn't have gone round seeking actual proof, as you've been doing. And I can't give it to you, as the only one who might have verified my story is no longer here.'

'You mean Colin.'

'Yes.' She didn't want to talk about Colin. For her the past proved only one thing, Paul's lack of faith in her. Sometimes a testing time comes before a relationship is actually formed. Maybe fate had been kind to her in a way. She might love Paul, but at least no one knew. She could never suffer the pain and humiliation of rejection for he had never accepted her.

'I think,' she allowed carefully, as he frowned broodingly, 'you have to love and respect someone before you can trust them completely. I'm not inclined to be suspicious of people, as you are, but sometimes I admit I do meet someone whom I instinctively dislike and distrust. That's probably what happened to you when you saw me, there doesn't always have to be a valid reason.'

There was silence. He did not answer and he made no move. The grey eyes assessed and examined, but there was no sign that he was impressed.

'Just what are you trying to prove, Jane?'

'Nothing,' she hesitated. 'Unless—that we should both go our separate ways.'

'After last night?'

Dry-mouthed and nervous, Jane drew a sharp breath. A flare of apprehension lit her mind, but she forced herself to speak rationally. 'I'm not what you think, Paul, but I'm not entirely naïve either. Put two people of opposite sex and compatible ages together, as we were a few hours ago, and anything can happen. It's biological.'

'I don't think so.'

'Well, anyway,' she swallowed, as his eyes darkened warningly, 'I believe we'd be wiser to forget.'

'Do you?'

She knew she was going to scream if she had to sit much longer, watching him watching her with that tigerish glint in his eyes. He was saying very little, but his expression terrified her. Quickly she glanced at her watch, praying she had time to get out before she lost control. It was getting more difficult by the minute to pretend a sophisticated indifference which didn't come naturally to her.

'The taxi must be waiting, Paul.' She reached for her cloak, her bag in her other hand. 'Oh,' she was walking towards the door when she paused in dismay, 'if your mother rings, what shall I tell her?'

'Tell her?' He had followed her. When she stopped so abruptly, he collided with her. It was so unexpected, it threw her off balance and his hands reached out to steady her as she stumbled. Lightly she was drawn against his hard, masculine body, then so close she felt his shape must be stamped on her back. He whirled her round with a sudden movement which made her head spin. She moaned in protest as his mouth came down, cruel and punishing against her lips. When he released her she was fighting to keep her sanity while every inch of her seemed on fire.

'Does that answer your question?' he asked sarcastically.

Jane thought she was too bruised to be able to work that day. Paul's voice floated somewhere above her. 'I was talking about your mother.'

'I wasn't,' he snapped, his eyes meeting her frightened blue ones. 'But since we've got one problem out the way, we can now, if you like.'

A wave of nausea hit her, but she had neither the nerve or strength to go into that again! If he thought he had won, she would just have to let him. Later she must think of some means of removing herself from his personal orbit—quietly, so he would never know she had gone until it was too late.

'Your mother——' she kept down the threatening sickness with difficulty. 'You promised we would go to Coombe Park this weekend. I want to know what I'm to say to her if she rings.'

'Tell her to speak to me,' he said, oddly remote but making it all sound extremely simple. 'I'll let you know.'

Was it so simple, or was he merely being clever? Jane wondered hollowly on reaching the studio an hour later. He would keep her on tenterhooks and she would worry all the time about what was going on. If she had been going to Coombe Park by herself, she could have relaxed and looked forward to it, but she had no idea whether Paul really intended going or not, and it might be the end of the week before he let her know anything definite.

London was still foggy that morning. At nine-thirty it was still murky. The streets and houses, huge stores and public buildings were just vague outlines wrapped in a gloom which showed no signs of lifting. For once Jane was glad that its depressing effect appeared to have spread to everyone in general. People were unobservant, huddled in warm clothes against the fog and cold. No one noticed she wasn't looking her best.

Mrs Banks had taken it for granted that Jane had spent the night with her friends. 'Wasn't the kind of weather you'd even put the cat out,' she had grumbled, happening to be on the doorstep fetching the milk when Jane arrived. Not for the first time Jane wished she hadn't gone out either!

Keith was the first to notice she was edgy. 'I'll have to take you out again,' he joked. 'Did wonders last time, remember?'

Jane did, but she didn't explain that it wasn't camera-shyness she was suffering from this time.

Keith took a closer look at her pale face and stopped teasing. 'A friend of mine is having an exhibition,' casually he named a leading art gallery. 'He sent me two first night tickets and I know he'd be delighted if you came with me. He's always telling me I should find myself a beautiful girl.'

Jane felt tired enough to drop. After a hard day's work she didn't think she would be looking very beautiful and she'd probably disgrace both herself and Keith by falling asleep. Yet wouldn't anything be better than sitting in her room, spending the long hours trying to solve unsolvable problems?

'I'd love to come, thank you, Keith,' she smiled, not realising until that moment that Paul was standing directly behind them.

After her first start of surprise she decided he had just

arrived. To her relief he merely nodded and said, 'Good morning, Jane,' as if he hadn't seen her since yesterday before turning to Keith.

To Keith he said, 'Stanburys have been in touch. There are a few things to sort out before I go to Australia next week.'

Stanburys, Jane knew, because by coincidence John Denyer had mentioned them last night, were one of the world's largest manufacturers, although the general public might not know their goods under that name. Their outlets were enormous, and apparently Paul had won their account in the face of fierce competition. They would be more important than Mrs Frey, though her business was important enough. She could understand why Keith had jumped.

With a rueful lift of his hand, he followed Paul out, leaving Jane wondering why she should be feeling despondent at having learned that Paul was going away. She was so busy thinking of this that she forgot to be curious as to why Paul had come himself for Keith when normally he would have left it to his secretary to find him.

They finished early as Mrs Frey was still undecided over the exact form of presentation for her new products. She was driving the copywriters mad while the typographers and designers were tearing their hair. It was the new perfume to go with the Spring collection which was causing the most bother. Its sales were to be assisted by TV commercials, and each time a layout was completed with its slogans and jingles, she changed her mind.

Jane hadn't seen Paul again all day, and his absence hadn't done her nerves any harm. When she reached home she felt relatively calm, especially as she had plenty of time to have a hot bath and a meal before meeting Keith. He had wanted to take her out for dinner, but he had been working late and had looked so harassed over the Stanburys account that she had taken pity on him and arranged to meet him later.

She wore her new fake fur coat, which she had bought with her first month's salary, over a silky calf-length dress. With her hair swept on top of her head and her face carefully made up, she didn't think she would let Keith down. She enjoyed touring the National and Tate Galleries but had never been to a private exhibition of art before. Pat had, once, and she had said everyone was terribly sophisticated and smart, but then Pat was fond of exaggerating.

She took a taxi, sighing at what she considered her growing extravagance but feeling unable to face the half mile walk to the tube. Deliberately she tried to concentrate on the lights of London instead of Paul, but the memory of the moments she had spent in his arms were difficult to dispel. It had been easier while she was working, but now images of her own abandonment returned to haunt her. She was determined to stay well away from him in future. He might be going to Australia, but he could be there and back in a week. As for spending this weekend at Coombe Park—she would ring his mother in the morning and simply say she couldn't make it and would come some other time.

When the taxi dropped her off in New Bond Street, Keith was waiting. Jane smiled at him when he told her she looked lovely.

'You sound as though you wished I didn't!' she teased.

'Self-protection,' he grinned. 'You're a temptation, but somehow I don't think you're for me.'

At the flicker of shrewdness at the back of his eyes, she flushed a little. 'How do you know?' she quipped, deliberately adopting a lightly flirtatious tone. At all costs, he mustn't discover she was in love with someone else.

'Sixth sense,' he replied, but so firmly that she looked quickly away.

Feeling somewhat chastened, she was silent as he found the building where the exhibition was being held and escorted her inside. Recognising the artist's name immediately she glanced around with awe. Jon Grice was one of the leading abstract painters of the day. Jane wasn't sure if she entirely understood the kind of thing he did, but she knew he was famous.

'Don't look so impressed,' Keith laughed. 'Such adulation could go to Jon's head.'

'He must be hardened to it by now,' Jane said dryly, not deaf to the general murmurs of appreciation.

John Grice's latest exhibition appeared to have floored even his most persistent of critics, for she heard not a single word of condemnation. She watched as he circled amongst his guests, a tall, thin man, perhaps in his late thirties. He seemed well liked, which she always judged was the mark of a pleasant personality. When the opportunity arose and Keith introduced her, she found nothing about him to alter this opinion.

He seemed as impressed by Jane as she was of him. 'I must paint you,' he said, staring at her closely, 'I shall probably make a mess of it but I must try.'

Having noticed all the beautiful women thronging the gallery, Jane put down his flattering remarks as a desire to please Keith. She was rather startled when he continued in this vein, his eyes still on her face.

'Such bone structure is rare.' Putting out a reverent hand, he tilted her chin. 'I'd like to do a profile— perfect! When could you sit for me?' he asked, clearly excited.

'Sorry, old man,' Keith at last intervened, 'Jane's working for International at the moment, under contract.'

'Which is for exclusive rights,' came Paul Denyer's voice, idle but with a hint of steel.

For the second time that day, Paul had caught her unawares. Startled, Jane swung round, then wished she hadn't when she saw the blonde vision clinging to his arm. Numbly she heard Jon replying to him.

'Good lord, Paul——' they obviously knew each other, 'I was thinking of our mutual pleasure, not advantage. She must be free at weekends. Why not let Jane decide?'

'Not this time,' Paul said coolly. 'And she already has arrangements for this weekend.'

Jane felt furious at his high-handedness. With another quick glance at the blonde she smiled at Jon warmly. 'My contract hasn't that long to run.'

'We must had dinner together one evening,' he smiled back, 'and discuss it.'

Jane thought Paul would move on, but he didn't. Instead, he introduced his girl-friend tersely. She wondered if he had meant to, or if he was merely using her to change the subject. Leonora Harding smiled vaguely at everyone without offering to shake hands. Jane thought sharply, she's frightened to take her hands off Paul for fear he escapes!

Jon Grice signalled a waiter. 'So many lovely ladies around,' he said gallantly, 'we must drink to them. It's generous of me, of course,' he added wryly, 'seeing how they're stealing my limelight! My next exhibition, I'm going to ban any female under fifty.'

Keith gave a shout of laughter. 'There'll be no women there!'

Jane listened to the lighthearted banter passing to and fro between Keith and Jon. It didn't bother her, but she found it impossible to join in. She was too aware of Leonora and Paul. It was the same girl, she realised, whom the media had snapped him with last week. It was absurd that she should feel a bitter pang of jealousy. Leonora was welcome to him!

It maddened her that she should suddenly feel very cold and miserable, wishing she could go home. Keith moved to let someone past and she found herself jammed against Paul.

'Not enjoying yourself, Miss Carey?' he muttered mockingly.

'Not as much as you are, I confess,' she whispered fiercely.

Jon begged Leonora the honour of showing her round. Clearly flattered, she went off with him, but not before entreating Paul not to run away. Someone hailed Keith and Jane was left feeling helplessly stranded and deserted.

'A cry for help might be misconstrued,' Paul taunted in her ear.

She wriggled painfully, her arm nearly breaking in the steely clasp of ruthless fingers. 'Do you think I'd care?'

'The publicity mightn't do you much good, unless it's any kind you're after?'

She glared at him, then glanced pointedly at her arm. 'Will you kindly let go of me!'

'Not before I speak to you.'

'What about?'

'About going out with another man, when I specifically told you not to!'

Incredulously, Jane's eyes widened. 'You have a nerve, attacking me like this, when you're out with another woman!'

'Leonora's different,' he snapped. 'We won't discuss her.'

Flushed and angry that he appeared to be putting Leonora on a pedestal, Jane hissed, 'You mean you wouldn't try and seduce her?'

'I wouldn't even think about it.'

'I suppose she's been selected as the future Mrs Denyer?' she cried, forcing herself to face the truth, doubting that Paul would spare her!

He didn't. 'She is,' he said.

Oh! Why had she been crazy enough to expect him to deny it? Her face went white and she swayed.

He had no pity that she was obviously in shock.

Catching hold of her by both arms this time, he shook her savagely. 'Never mind,' he said, his eyes smouldering, 'concentrate on the great things which could happen when you leave International. Grice wants to paint you and you're certainly a superb actress. I've never met anyone so able to change colour at will. You'll probably be auditioned on the strength of your commercials alone.'

'You think you can read me like a book, don't you,' she cried angrily, 'but I'm the only one who can do that—and my version and yours are entirely different! And if I don't always understand myself,' she raced on rashly, 'I certainly understand you! You're the kind of man who uses his wife to decorate his front parlour while he amuses himself with his mistress in the attic.'

'You're impertinent, Miss Carey!'

'I'm honest!' She didn't care if he was black with rage.

'Do you really believe it?'

Jane didn't realise they were beginning to attract attention, that people were glancing at them curiously. Keith, fortunately, noticed and returned quickly to Jane's side.

'Time we were leaving, sweetheart,' he said lightly. 'Let's find somewhere to eat, unless you'd rather go to my place or your own.'

'I'll collect Leonora.' Paul shot him a stony glance. 'I have a table already booked, so you can join us. Otherwise you won't find much going spare at this time of night. You may as well ask Grice if he'd like to come along later. It's a pity his wife isn't here.'

'Why didn't you refuse?' Jane mumbled to Keith as they climbed in the back of Paul's car.

'Why didn't you?' he enquired in a dry whisper.

'He bulldozes people. Someone ought to stop him.'

'He's the boss, love,' Keith shrugged. 'At least, I consider he's mine, and I have a healthy respect both for him and the salary he pays.'

'Because he knows you're the best,' she said sharply, trying not to stare at Leonora huddled against Paul, seeking comfort like a cat. How was he managing to drive? she wondered, feeling weighed down with misery.

'No one believed it till he did,' Keith retorted.

In the nightclub, where they ate a light supper, Paul looked after Leonora as though she was a precious gem entrusted to his keeping. How he managed to watch herself like a hawk at the same time was beyond Jane.

On the whole it proved a pleasant enough evening; she knew she had no excuse for not enjoying it. The conversation flowed smoothly—although there was one awkward moment while Jon Grice's paintings were being discussed and Keith happened to remark that being separated from his wife didn't appear to have affected his style very much. To which Paul replied curtly, with a sharp glance at Jane, that as far as he was aware the split wasn't permanent, and, barring outside interference, Jon's wife had every hope of a reconciliation.

Paul didn't ask Jane to dance, but Keith did. So did Jon when he arrived. She danced with him once, and with Paul's icy eyes on her as they jostled in the limited space, she had no wish to repeat the experience. He could make her tremble just by looking at her, and she realised he knew it.

'Leonora doesn't seem his type,' she said to Keith, as she danced with him a second time.

'Every woman thinks that,' he teased, 'when they see him with someone else.'

Jane regretted saying anything. If she was green with envy it wasn't Leonora's fault. On the whole she seemed a very nice girl, and if she was smothering Paul—well, he must have given her every encouragement!

'I get the impression you've met before,' Jane said carefully.

'Once or twice,' he confessed with a grin. 'She's not so naïve as she seems—but harmless, of course.'

'Is that all?'

'Now who's being bitchy?' he laughed.

They stayed until the early hours. Keith and Jon might have been inclined to leave sooner, but because Paul didn't make a move they lazily stayed on. They went down to the casino where the two girls watched the three men lose and then win a handful of money.

Paul asked Leonora if she'd like to try her luck, but she went into a helpless flutter. When she coyly shook her head and fluttered her false eyelashes at him, Jane couldn't restrain a flicker of contempt.

On realising Paul had seen it, she wished she had merely looked the other way, and flushed with alarm as he didn't ask but insisted she played.

While she was still searching wildly for some means of extricating herself, he forced her down into the seat he had just vacated, holding her there by the weight of his hands on her shoulders. Nor did he release her, despite Leonora's sulky glances, until she had lost what she anxiously calculated must be about the equivalent of a week's salary.

As she had very little money with her, she was forced to suffer the shameful embarrassment of allowing him to settle her debts. 'I'll keep it off your wages,' he said suavely, as if she was a careless kitchenmaid he had caught breaking dishes.

As the others murmured sympathetically, without apparently taking the incident at all seriously, Jane stared at him mutinously, wondering what sort of game he was playing. Surely one woman was enough for him to torment, she thought angrily, glancing, with a sympathy that surprised her, at Leonora's unhappy face.

CHAPTER NINE

JANE was still thinking unpleasant things about him when Paul waylaid her, next morning, on her way to work. She almost groaned aloud when she saw him. While there was a lot she had to say to him, things she hadn't had the chance to say the evening before, there was nothing that wouldn't keep. With a heavy day in front of her, he was the last person on earth she wanted to see. She felt herself beginning to tremble, something which always seemed to happen when Paul was around, and she stared at him despairingly, feeling like bursting into frustrated tears.

He looked haggard, she noticed. The course of true love mustn't be running smoothly for him, either! Swiftly she lowered her lashes to hide a fleeting but empty satisfaction.

The corridor was deserted, they had it all to themselves. For a change, she thought bleakly, Paul must like the idea of there being no one about to witness him grinding away at her nerves!

'Good morning,' his eyes flicked coolly over her strained face. 'I spoke to my mother last night. You're to go on Friday evening, for the weekend.'

Jane started. As usual he had been too clever for her! He had said he would ring his mother, but she had decided he wouldn't. Because of this, she had imagined she had enough time to get in touch with Mrs Denyer herself. Now he had beaten her to it and made arrangements which would be embarrassing to break. Well, she would go on her own, gladly, but not with him!

'Did you intend coming with me?' she asked carefully.

'No.'

'Oh . . .' She blinked at him uncertainly, realising she had expected him to say yes.

A mocking smile quirked his lips. 'Surprised you, have I?'

She had to deny it, of course, but she knew he didn't believe her. 'Nothing about you surprises me any more.'

'Pity,' he drawled, then, quite curtly, 'I take it you will be going?'

Suddenly she was tired of fencing with him. Her blue eyes wide, she appealed to him, 'Would you really mind if I spent the weekend with your parents, Paul? You've been so against it, I mean . . .'

'I know exactly what you mean.'

She nodded. 'You've been so absolutely against it.'

'Perhaps I've decided it's easier to swim with the tide than against it. Sometimes you can reach your goal quicker that way.'

'Leonora appears to think so.'

'Bitch!'

Despair still carrying her recklessly, she rushed on, 'I imagine you'll be spending the weekend in her company?'

'Naturally.'

Hoping it was disdain in her eyes rather than tears, Jane glared at him. What wouldn't she give to wipe that arrogant expression off his face!

'You look very fetching when you're thinking of ways to annihilate me,' he taunted.

'I hate you,' she whispered.

'Prove it.' Silkily Paul pulled her into his arms, his eyes darkening as he lowered his head, his intentions obvious.

'No!' Her strangled gasp was audible but ineffectual. Realising this, she struggled frantically. She wasn't going to be caught grovelling at his feet, as he had threatened, and she knew what his kisses could do to her. He had imprisoned her heart, now even her mind seemed in danger of surrendering. In a turmoil of resentment she hit out at him. As her nails caught his cheek, he released her, cursing loudly.

His secretary appeared at his office door, her glance alive with curiosity. 'You're required urgently, Mr Denyer. New York.'

'Hell!' His eyes scorched her, glittering with fury. 'Can't you see I'm not available?'

'I'm sorry, Mr Denyer.'

'Tell them I'll be there in a minute,' he rasped.

As the woman swallowed palely and retreated, Jane felt sorry for her. She hoped Miss Dalton realised she wasn't responsible for Paul's temper.

'Don't let me stop you,' she mumbled unhappily, viewing his torn face, her own white.

Catching her off guard, he grabbed her again, roughly taking her hand, placing it against his bleeding skin. 'Savage!' he bit out as she stared at the trickle of blood on her palm. 'I should make you taste it!'

'Oh, Paul!' She really did feel full of remorse, discovering you couldn't love someone and enjoy wounding them. He hurt her all the time—but then he didn't love her. In his heart she was mixed up with his brother's death, and each time he looked at her he was remembering, hating her. Hating her, too, that she attracted him physically. Leonora's influence wasn't apparently strong enough to render him indifferent. He would resent that as well.

'Kiss me better,' he said thickly, clearly out for revenge.

Blindly she obeyed, no longer seeking to understand herself or him as her lips found his cheek before sliding involuntarily to his mouth. Not a muscle of his face moved, but she felt a deep shudder run right through him.

Abruptly he lifted his head, pushing her away, his eyes half hidden under heavy lids. Turning from her, he muttered grimly, 'I'll see you later, Miss Carey.'

All day he intruded on Jane's thoughts, however hard she tried not to let him. Why did he have to taunt her, haunt her so, when he was in love with another woman? For reasons best known to himself, he was keeping quiet regarding his future plans, not yet ready, seemingly, to announce his engagement. When he did, Jane knew life for her would go on but mightn't be worth living.

Paul sent word that he was tied up, but if he didn't see her before she left, he would call at her flat; she wasn't to go out. The message was delivered by a typist who didn't even bother to lower her voice.

Jane was having her coffee break, with Keith sitting beside her. Feeling forced to say something, when the girl departed, she muttered tersely, 'He sounds busy!'

She was aware of Keith's eyes on her hot cheeks as his brows rose quizzically. 'He's still dealing with Stanburys.'

'I thought that had been sorted out?'

'Nothing in this game is ever completely sorted out,' Keith sighed. 'There are always problems.'

'Can Paul cope if there's real trouble?' she frowned.

'Cope?' Keith laughed, unusually incredulous. 'That guy can cope with anything! To say he has genius is an understatement. Stanburys are eating out of his hand.'

'How nice for him!' Jane sought to cover her mistaken anxiety with tartness.

'Tut, tut, girl,' Keith grinned, 'methinks you protest too much!'

Jane tilted her chin, in no mood to be teased, momentarily deprived of a sense of humour. 'What about his brother?' she asked shortly. 'Doesn't he deserve any credit?'

Keith shrugged. 'As a plodder, a carrier out of orders, maybe. On his own he could never have made it. Neither would the youngest brother—well, I won't go into that, but they all rely—relied—on Paul.'

'His father must have passed on a nice business, though?'

'The foundations of one, I agree,' Keith mused, 'but it's Paul who's built it up to what it is today. International's only become international since he took over.'

If Jane couldn't really feel surprised at what she heard, she wasn't willing to appear impressed. She objected to the way in which Paul had ordered her to wait in her flat for him, though she couldn't help wondering what he wanted to see her about. Probably only to torment her some more, she decided wearily.

The hours she spent just holding a pose provided ample opportunity for thought, and she pondered on the changes in Paul since she had known him. She had seen so many different sides to his personality and still had no idea which was the real one. There was the man by her hospital bed, cool, authoritative, older, letting her cling while managing to remain remote. He had answered a need in her but retained his own individuality, the hunger she had occasionally surprised in him, surely a reflection of her own. At Coombe Park, he had changed again, from a casual friend to a startlingly determined lover. She hadn't got used to coping with the latter when her memory returned and she had been exposed to the unleashed torture of his savage condemnation. Since then, he had moved to a refinement of torture she found difficult to comprehend. Very likely, at this moment, he was sitting in his office conjuring up other ways of making her suffer.

To her relief there was no sign of him when it was time to go home. As she left the building, Ben Dufton, one of the photographers, caught up with her, his method of approach making it obvious that he had pursued her deliberately.

'How about a drink?' he invited casually, then grinned as she was clearly thinking of a way to refuse politely. 'I'm not asking for a date, darling, much as I'd like to. I've one or two suggestions to make—nice ones,' he added hastily, wryly nodding in the direction of the offices, 'and it's difficult, in there, to get a word with you alone.'

Jane didn't need a drink, but she saw no harm in popping into a nearby coffee shop with him for half an hour. Suddenly she saw Ben as the excuse she had been looking for not to go home. Later she might go to the cinema, but in the meantime, what had she to lose by listening to what he had to say?

As it happened, he merely wanted to know if she had any plans for the future, once her present contract ran out. She hadn't, but she was strangely reluctant to commit herself even as far as confessing that.

'I'm not sure what I'll be doing,' she said, softening what she suspected might be an irritating vagueness with a gentle smile.

If Ben was irritated he hid it well. It appeared he had a cousin who did freelance fashion photography and, like many others, was particularly interested in new faces. Jane assured him she would think about it, while refusing to promise anything.

Once this had been suggested, she saw no reason to linger, but Ben begged her not to hurry away. Because the coffee shop was warm and he was entertaining, she gave in. He began talking about his career, dropping a few professional hints which she knew, as a model, she should be storing as invaluable. He wasn't in the least like the licentious photographer who had accompanied her to Italy, and she was amazed to consult her watch and discover that two hours had passed in a flash.

'I must be going!' she said in surprise.

'Why not have dinner with me?' he grinned. 'No strings.'

She almost agreed again, driven by a curious recklessness, until her innate sense of caution stopped her. 'Another time, perhaps,' she smiled, and left him.

Deciding to stick to her original plan, she went to the

Odeon and saw a film she had wanted to see for ages. She even thought of having something to eat when she came out, but by the time the show was over her appetite had disappeared and she decided to go straight home. When she got there it was almost twelve, and trying not to wonder if Paul had called, she had a quick bath and crept into bed.

She didn't discover whether he had called or not, as whenever she caught sight of him, during the next few days, he appeared to be looking the other way. Friday evening arrived after a space of relative calm. Jane felt impatient with herself for imagining apprehensively that it was the kind of calm which frequently presages a storm. Paul had asked to see her, but he might easily have changed his mind. She tried to assure herself it was the sort of thing he did without a thought for other people's feelings—so why should she worry over his!

On Friday, when she didn't see him at all, she heaved a sigh of relief as she returned home to pick up her case and wait for the Denyers to collect her. Somehow, all week, she had feared she might be dragged into Paul's office and given a lecture on disobeying orders which might be capable of shattering her hard won composure.

It calmed her, too, that there should be a letter waiting for her from Beth, though the news it contained was both delightful and worrying. Beth wrote that she was pregnant and suffering terribly from morning sickness, which was why she hadn't got down to see Jane.

'We're both delighted about the baby,' she went on, 'and our doctor promises I'll almost certainly begin feeling better, but he advises against travelling far until I do. Anyway, Tom won't hear of it. Instead he suggests you come up here and visit us. I'd love to see you, Jane ...' to Jane it seemed Beth was almost begging, 'Tom's a darling and so good to me, but sometimes

I think I'd give anything for the sight of a familiar female face. Especially yours!'

Jane was about to pick up a pen to reply to Beth's letter before she began packing and changing, when suddenly she hesitated. After offering her congratulations, she had intended explaining how she couldn't possibly get away, but suddenly she wondered, why shouldn't she? Beth was the only family she had ever known and they loved each other like sisters. Surely if she talked to Mrs Frey, she would agree to releasing her for even a short period. Mrs Frey was first and foremost a business woman, but she was also a woman of rare understanding. Jane decided it might at least be worth waiting to see.

Despite Beth's assurances that she would be all right, Jane worried about her all the way to Coombe Park, which helped strengthen her resolve to ask Mrs Frey for some time off. Meanwhile, she thought, if the opportunity arose, she might ask Mrs Denyer if she knew of anything which might help Beth's morning sickness. She just might, as she had had three children of her own.

At Coombe Park, Jane found a warm welcome waiting her, and, as always, she was aware of a sense of peace. There being no sign of Paul, she felt a twinge of guilt for doubting he would keep his word and stay away. There were two other guests staying, unexpected visitors from abroad, Mrs Denyer whispered, but Jane liked them and the evening passed pleasantly. In fact, the whole weekend promised to be pleasant, which did nothing to prepare her for the shock she received the next day.

The following morning she was given her breakfast in bed by a fussing Mrs Finn, who declared she was looking far too pale and thin. Much as Jane enjoyed such pampering, for a change, she was sure a few hours' fresh air would do her more good. Afterwards, in a pair of jeans and old sweater, she roamed with the dogs, returning regrettably untidy but feeling more relaxed than she had done for weeks. Hoping she wasn't late for lunch and holding everyone up, she put on an extra spurt as she rounded the corner of the house, and almost fell over Paul. He was helping James unload a set of expensive luggage from his car, watched by a helplessly fluttering Leonora.

As Jane's racing feet skidded on the gravel, Paul turned abruptly to steady her. Dropping the case he held, he grasped her arms. 'Just what do you think you're doing?' he snapped.

Jane felt the drive heave and spin as she swayed. Briefly she closed her eyes, unaware of the despair in them when she managed to open them again. 'You said you weren't coming!' she breathed.

'I said I wasn't coming with you,' he retorted coolly.

As their eyes met, she knew a wild sense of anger. He was such a devious twister of words. She might have guessed! 'You gave the impression——' she began hotly.

'I can't be responsible if you got the wrong one,' he cut in, 'and what I choose to do is really no concern of yours. Where the hell have you been, anyway?' His cold glance swept sharply over the tangled hair tumbling untidily about her head. 'You look a sight!'

At that moment, fortunately, Mrs Denyer came hurrying from the front door. With a warm smile, she embraced Leonora, kissing her lightly. 'I'm so sorry, dear, I didn't hear you arrive. Welcome to Coombe Park.'

As Paul let her go, to speak to his mother, Jane heard Leonora thanking her sweetly. 'I'm so pleased to be here.'

Jane bent to stroke Thor, her face white. How could Paul do this to her? She had seen his hand resting briefly on Leonora's waist before he concentrated again on the luggage. There was such a pile of it, she wondered if the other girl intended staying here permanently.

Giving Thor a final pat, she tried to slink invisibly past the other two women, but to her dismay Mary caught her arm.

'Jane, I'd like you to meet . . .'

'We've already met,' Jane interrupted, she feared rudely, but quite unable to help herself.

'Oh!' Mary sounded surprised but quickly recovered. 'Then you'll know she's going to be my daugher-in-law? I'd almost stopped hoping for one.'

'Oh, Mrs Denyer!' Leonora smirked, laying a hand adorned by an outsize diamond on Mary's arm.

Behind them, Paul asked lazily, 'Any chance of an early lunch? I'm famished!'

Jane turned and fled, finding herself in her room without any clear idea of how she'd got there. So it had happened. With tears streaming down her cheeks, she flung herself on her bed. Oh, God, she sobbed, how did one survive something like this? Remembering where she was, she tried desperately to pull herself together, but when self-reasoning had no effect, she clumsily tore off her clothes and dived under the shower. Eventually this did the trick. A few minutes later, her sobs having subsided to a painful hiccuping, she began to dress.

She found a soft skirt with a long-sleeved blouse and toning gilet in neutral shades of tan and orange which seemed to lend her face a little colour. Brushing the tangles from her hair, she left it falling loosely in shining waves, not having the heart to do anything elaborate with it. She only applied the faintest hint of make-up to hide the redness round her eyes. No one would be looking at her anyway, they would be too busy concentrating on Paul's future bride.

She wished she had had the courage to leave the house straight away. When she did she knew she would never come back, but it was pride, not nostalgia, that drove her downstairs again. She was late, and no one seemed to mind when she refused the champagne with which the others were toasting a radiant Leonora. For once Jane seemed to have timed things perfectly, for when she arrived the company gravitated immediately towards the dining room.

The quivering inside her was gradually overtaken by a frozen feeling, a welcome numbness, stiffening her unsteady limbs. She was even able to note dispassionately that it was a strange meal, with Paul and his father talking high finance with the overseas visitors, without taking a great deal of interest as Leonora discussed her wedding dress with Mary. Jane listened, but with Paul's gaze frequently switching to her, she found it almost impossible to contribute much to the general conversation.

Between Paul's calculating glances and Leonora's nonstop chatter, her nerves grew so taut she feared they might snap. Leonora was having her wedding dress made in Paris, there being apparently no lack of funds in her titled family.

'Paris was where I first met Paul,' she leaned eagerly across the table towards him, 'wasn't it, darling?'

Jane's smothered gasp couldn't have been audible, but his eyes swung to her briefly, as though he enjoyed her discomfort. Smiling at Leonora, he confessed blandly, 'That's right. I was quite bowled over.'

So now she knew, Jane thought bitterly, watching the teasing warmth on his face. And it was something she was going to have to learn to accept. He and Leonora had met in Paris, fallen in love and would shortly be married. Suddenly she had no appetite for lunch and hoped miserably that no one would notice she was merely playing with the food on her plate.

Later in the afternoon, Mary suggested they all had a short stroll in the park before tea, but Leonora protested that she didn't much like walking and would rather stay indoors and watch T.V. Paul offered to stay with her, much to Jane's relief, as she was unable to think of anything she'd like better than to get away from him for a while, but, to her despair, all the time she was out, she found she couldn't stop picturing him with Leonora in his arms, making love to her before the warm intimacy of the drawing-room fire.

As Mary and John Denyer, believing Jane to be fully entertained by the antics of the dogs, chatted to their other guests, she had plenty of time to ponder. What had made Paul fall in love with a girl like Leonora? She was certainly pretty but could never be described as over-intelligent. When Jane had first met her, at Jon Grice's exhibition, she had believed she was spiteful, but since meeting her a second time, Jane realised she was thoughtless, rather than vindictive. She had obviously been spoiled, which had made her completely self-centred and insensitive to other people's feelings. Yet there was a naïveté about her which Jane found oddly attractive and she imagined, if Paul continued spoiling her a little, Leonora might make him a sweetly amenable wife. Which was, she reflected moodily, what most men wanted anyway.

Jane thrust the terms sugary and passionless from her mind. If Leonora appeared to dislike being touched or having a hair out of place—well, what of it? She was well connected and in this sense alone would be able to help Paul much more than someone like herself, a girl from an orphanage ever could.

On returning to the house, she asked Mary if she would mind if she skipped tea as she had a letter to write. This was partly true as she had decided to start a letter to Beth which she could finish quickly after consulting Mrs Frey on Monday and hearing her decision. She was aware that Mary was slightly puzzled by her behaviour, but she couldn't tell her that her main reason for missing tea was that she wanted to avoid her son. She would have to appear for dinner, but at least that would give her some respite.

On her way to her room, she heaved a wry sigh on realising that since she had eaten no lunch and had refused coffee, one of the things she most longed for was a cup of tea. Regretting how she couldn't ignore her physical needs for ever, she turned and went quickly to the rear of the house and from there down the back stairs to the kitchens. When she had stayed at Coombe Park, as Colin's wife, she had frequently used the back stairs during the nights when she couldn't sleep in order to make herself a hot drink.

Mrs Finn frowned but didn't say much as Jane produced a somewhat halting explanation. She made her sit at the big scrubbed table and after pouring two cups of tea, sat down beside her.

'You may as well have some biscuits as well,' she pushed a plateful towards her. 'Not too many, mind,' she warned, as though Jane was ten years old, 'or you'll spoil your dinner!'

Jane had to pretend she was exercising great control when she could scarcely manage one. The maids were eager to hear about her modelling career, and she was just beginning to tell them it wasn't as glamorous as it was generally believed to be, when Paul walked in.

'Hello, Mrs Finn,' his mouth twisted sardonically, 'aren't you flattered that Miss Carey has deserted the drawing-room in your favour?'

Mrs Finn glanced at him reproachfully but was wise enough to know he wasn't getting at her. 'Now, Mr Paul . . .!' she began.

Taking no notice, he picked up a biscuit and Jane's cup of tea. 'Come along, Jane,' he said curtly, 'I'll carry this upstairs for you. I want to talk to you.'

While resenting such high-handedness, Jane could only stare at him numbly as she scrambled to her feet and followed him from the room. She suspected she might be outdoing Leonora for mindlessness as she almost ran to keep up with him.

'What will Mrs Finn think?' she gasped.

'You might be surprised,' he snapped back.

'I don't know what you can have to say that can't

wait!' she panted behind him, as he took the stairs two at a time.

In her bedroom he closed the door behind them, then put her cup down grimly. 'You like keeping me waiting, don't you?' he rasped. 'The other day when I sent word that I wanted to speak to you, you ditched me in favour of Ben Dufton.'

As she started, he jeered, 'That shook you, did it?'

'How did you find out?' she whispered, realising she wasn't helping herself by sounding so guilty.

'I followed you, didn't I!' he muttered savagely. 'But you were so engrossed, you didn't see a taxi almost mow me down.'

She could imagine. No taxi would dare! A little of her courage returned. 'Ben had something to ask me,' she said.

'And you said yes, I presume!'

She refused to be intimidated by his gibes any longer. 'Don't you think you ought to be getting back to Leonora?' She couldn't being herself to say—your fiancée. The word stuck in her throat.

'She won't be taking any harm.'

'She's bound to be missing you, though.'

His grey eyes were indifferent. 'She'll soon learn I like my—er—little diversions.'

Jane drew a furious breath. 'You make me sick!'

'Is that all?' Derisively, Paul suddenly took hold of her, pulling her close, making her look at him. As their eyes met, an explosion of awareness shot through Jane like a forest fire, making her senses sing and her heart beat so fast she thought she was in danger of suffocating. The early autumn darkness had reduced the light to dimness in the silent room, yet she seemed to see every inch of his hard, handsome features with amazing clarity.

Why did he have to appeal to her the way he did? she wondered dazedly. Why could she resist his dark magnetism no more than she could deny her shameful longing to belong to him completely? Anger stirred inside her, both at the way he treated her and her own inability to retaliate. She was unable to move as his mouth crushed hers in a ruthless kiss. Summoning all her strength, she tried to push him away, but his hands tightened on her slender waist, securing her firmly.

'Jane,' he muttered thickly, against the stubborn resistance of her lips, 'why won't you give in to me?'

Blindly she shook her head, terrified that he might guess how much she was tempted to. 'What did you want to see me about?' she whispered.

He kissed the tip of her nose with a patience she found somehow frightening, before his mouth trailed to her throat, resting with a curve of satisfaction on the racing pulse. 'Disobeying orders, for one thing.'

'Disobeying orders?' she repeated, confused.

'Going out with other men. Keith—Ben . . .'

His voice was growing abstracted and she didn't reply. She felt she was moving into a kind of trance. Heat rose in her body as the fight went out of her and his lips returned to capture hers. Gently his hands found their way under her thin blouse, seductively caressing her silky skin until she didn't know how much more she could endure. His mouth was firm and compelling, and an awful wanton weakness possessed her, silencing her conscience. Moaning weakly, she pressed her fingers in his thick black hair, bring his lips fully down on her parted ones.

When his mouth began exploring deeply and urgently, she wanted all he was prepared to give. Suddenly she forgot all about Leonora and just wanted him to take and take. She allowed him to continue making love to her, clinging to him helplessly, telling him without words how much she needed him. Slowly, with a harsh rasp of breath, he lowered her to the floor, making no attempt to disguise the desire which was running in him just as passionately.

The buttons of his shirt parted as her arms slipped

inside to wrap round his waist, as he came down beside her. He took it off, then lifted her slightly to remove her own clothing. While he undressed her, they seemed to be elevated to an entirely different plane, one where words and actions were directed by a force over which they had no control. If his movements were lacking their customary deftness Jane was unaware of it. She was only conscious of the shudders running strongly through him and of her own feverish response.

Holding her against the bareness of his chest, he slid her skirt over her hips. At the exquisite contact, flames ignited inside her and she clutched at him helplessly. His fingers pushed gently into the waistband of her satin panties, causing her heart to throb with excitement as he took them off. 'You're beautiful,' he murmured huskily, pushing her back to the floor. As they lay naked, Paul kissing her, Jane could feel the sweat, pouring between their tensely waiting bodies.

His fingers lightly caressed the swell of her hips as his mouth found her white breasts. The nipples were taut and he teased them with his teeth until she cried out. Fire raged through her blood as she pressed hot lips to the side of his neck and felt his urgent reaction. Blindly, scarcely realising what she was doing, she let her hands wander over him, gripping painfully as he overwhelmed her time and again with the evidence of his growing arousal. Her eyes were glazed by the depth of her own sensuality as she watched the blood beat in his temple and the ache in the pit of her stomach expanded to consume every part of her.

Somehow, from somewhere, when the volume of feeling grew unsupportable, she found the strength to protest, but Paul took no notice.

'Too late!' she heard him gasp. 'You can't back out now.'

Not giving her a chance to answer, his mouth ground hard against hers, and his body pressed painfully over her own. Everything began swimming about her as she felt she was falling into a timeless volcanic void of indescribable pleasure.

Then the sound of voices and laughter intruded. People could be heard talking loudly. There was a heavy thumping and playful barking from the corridor and upper hall, and as she felt Paul stir to a kind of frozen stillness, Jane realised the dogs must have escaped their usual quarters and were leading the maids a fine old dance outside.

With an explosive curse of frustration, Paul rolled away from her and jumped to his feet. Opening dazed eyes, Jane felt herself shrink at the expression of disgust on his face. Her cheeks scorched as she watched him throw on his discarded clothing and slip swiftly from the room, all without once looking at her.

She could have been half dead or hurt, but he hadn't cared enough to spare the time even to enquire! Moving more clumsily, she gathered up her own clothes, just managing to reach her bathroom before someone knocked.

It was Wendy, one of the maids, explaining, unnecessarily, Jane thought, what had happened, and apologising if the noise had disturbed her. Jane, pretending she was about to take a shower, thanked her and managed to add that she hoped the dogs hadn't caused too much bother.

She took a bath, not a shower, after Wendy had gone, deriving some comfort, if only physically from the warm, soothing water and tried not to think of what had happened. She wasn't sure if she felt more horrified by her own behaviour or Paul's. If she felt sorry for anyone it was Leonora. If Paul couldn't be faithful before marriage, what sort of husband would he make? Somehow Jane knew she must endeavour, for her own sake as much as Leonora's, to remove herself from his presence, which might mean leaving International, if she possibly could. Perhaps Mrs Frey would allow her to work somewhere else, if she could think of a suitable and convincing explanation.

Jane lingered as long as she dared in her room before going down to dinner. She was wearing a white jersey dress with gold, high-heeled sandals. The dress had a low, scooped neckline which showed to advantage her long neck and nicely sloped shoulders, but she was vaguely dissatisfied with her reflection, So much pale colour, she thought, made her look too ethereal and she wished she had brought something brighter, like the blouse she had worn for lunch.

The evening must have been a great success, judging by the happy expressions on the faces of the other guests, but Jane never knew how she got through it. She found it difficult to take her eyes off Paul, he seemed to absorb her senses to the exclusion of everything else. In dark trousers and jacket setting off every powerful line of his tall, lean figure, she was constantly aware of him and the tension between them which occasionally held her breathless and feeling rooted to the spot.

Returning to the drawing-room for coffee, she was startled to hear his voice behind her, saying thickly, 'I have to speak to you, Jane. Will you come outside?'

'No!' she gasped, wondering how he had the nerve, and knowing she could never trust herself alone with him again.

'You have to listen,' he snatched her arm, his face taut and strained. 'You must realise how serious the situation is! We have to do something about it.'

'Please just leave me alone!' she cried desperately. 'Paul!'

Neither of them had noticed Mary Denyer right behind them. She must have overheard every word of their bitter exchange. 'You're making so much noise . . .' Clearly embarrassed, she threw up her hands helplessly as the others began appearing.

'Oh, hell!' With a smothered curse, Paul swung on his heel, his glance savage on Jane's white face. 'All right, if

you won't come with me, I'll find someone who will!'
With an indifferent shrug, he turned to ask a smiling
Leonora if she felt like going out somewhere for the rest
of the evening.

CHAPTER TEN

THE following morning, because of Paul, Jane lingered late in her room, hoping to avoid him. To her relief there was no sign of him, and she had just finished breakfast and was leaving the dining-room when his mother caught up with her.

'Good morning, dear' her eyes went anxiously to Jane's wary face. 'I'm afraid Paul's had to leave the country unexpectedly, but he left this for you.'

While she explained something about trouble in the New York office, Jane stared uncertainly at the note she had been given and finally opened it.

He had obviously been short of time. 'I must talk to you, Jane,' he wrote swiftly. 'I'll call you on Tuesday evening as soon as my flight gets in.'

Jane read the note through twice, feeling suddenly terribly shaken. She forgot there was someone with her until Mary spoke again.

'What is it, dear?' she frowned uneasily. 'You've gone quite white.'

'Nothing. That is, nothing much. Paul—oh, it doesn't matter!' Jane faltered, horrified to find tears springing to her eyes and humiliatingly conscious that Mary had seen them.

Mary hesistated, clearly deciding not to probe any further. 'He shouldn't be away very long,' she said vaguely.

Grateful for such restraint, Jane managed a brief nod. 'I'll have to leave too, I think, although,' she forced herself to add lightly, 'not for anywhere as exciting as New York!'

Mary glanced at her in dismay. 'You mean you want to go home? Oh, dear,' she exclaimed, 'do you have to?

I realise this weekend hasn't been much fun for you. What with Leonora and Malcolm and Jean arriving as they did, I've hardly seen anything of you.'

'No, it's not that!' impulsively Jane gave her a quick, adoring hug. 'You've been more than kind, only there are things I must see to.'

'And you believe because we have other company we won't miss you?' Mary smiled at her affectionately. 'You must know we always do. You'll have to come for another weekend soon.'

Jane thanked her, feeling unable to hurt Mary, especially at that moment, by trying to explain that she doubted if she could ever bring herself to return to Coombe Park again, even for a short visit.

Mary sighed regretfully. 'Well, dear, I won't insist you stay longer if you feel you can't. James will drive you to your flat, whenever you wish to go.'

Thanking her again, Jane was turning away to go upstairs and get her things, when she suddenly remembered something she had been going to ask. 'Oh, please, Mrs Denyer,' she said quickly, 'do you know of a cure for morning sickness? I have a friend . . .'

Her voice broke off as Mary went pale, and Jane knew she must be thinking of Colin. Aghast that she could have been so insensitive, she was even more dismayed when the drawing-room door opened and Leonora approached them.

'I'm sorry,' she said hastily, 'please don't give it another thought—the doctor is sure it will pass.'

Mary nodded dumbly and Jane didn't speak to her alone again before she left. There was only a moment, as she said goodbye with the others looking on, that Mary whispered, 'Do remember, if you're ever in need of help, come to me.'

The flat seemed cold and empty after the warmth and comfort of the house she had just left. She hadn't been in five minutes when Mrs Banks appeared, to tell her that a lady had called and left a number for Jane to ring back.

'She said it were urgent,' Mrs Banks grumbled, manoeuvring her large protesting body downstairs again.

At first Jane thought it must be Beth, but on hurrying to the phone she discovered it was a London number and Mrs Frey. Mrs Frey's husband had been French and apparently one of his sisters had died. Jane wondered what this could have to do with her until Mrs Frey explained.

'Apart from the funeral there'll be private matters to attend to, and as I shall be gone several days, I've arranged for you to take the week off as well.'

Could she do that? It might be the answer to her prayers, but what about International? The Frey account was theirs. Mrs Frey said she had arranged for her to have time off, but Jane wondered if they knew anything about it.

'Are you sure it will be all right with International?'

'Yes, of course!' Mrs Frey replied impatiently. 'You know how important the layout for my new cosmetics is to me, Jane! I have to be there each day. So if we both disappear nothing can be changed behind my back and there's absolutely nothing they can do about it. I'll see they don't lose by it, anyway.'

Jane frowned as Mrs Frey bade her a swift farewell. Mrs Frey had never learned to delegate, and the explanation she had given was far from satisfactory, but suddenly Jane decided to take her at her word. Why look a gift horse in the mouth? she thought defiantly. Hadn't she been going to ask for a few days off to see Beth? And if she was dismissed for it—well, what of it? It might be the best thing that could happen, seeing how desperate she was to leave International?

She left the next morning for Scotland, catching a train to Glasgow at ten. She could have left earlier, but she wanted to buy something for Beth. In a famous store she found two gay smocks which she knew Beth would love, and a new book, just out, by Tom's favourite author. She also bought a good luck token for the house as this would be her first visit. Knowing what her friends liked made shopping for them easy, but nevertheless, it proved a rush. She was breathless long before she reached the station and still not sure that she was doing the right thing. She was determined to see Beth, but at the same time she suspected she was running from Paul like a coward. Yet what would be the point of staying and meeting him again, now that she had indisputable proof that he loved another girl?

By sheer good luck, on reaching Glasgow, she managed to connect with a flight for the Shetlands, where Beth's husband held an executive position with the oil company he worked for. Some three hours later she arrived.

The islands looked wild and lonely and very beautiful in the fading light of the late autumn afternoon. Such stark beauty caught at Jane's throat and she gazed in awe at their wind and sea-tossed grandeur before the plane lost height to land on the runway.

Beth and Tom, whom she had contacted briefly the previous evening, and who had given her detailed instructions on how to get there, were there to meet her.

'Oh, darling!' Beth flung her arms around Jane rapturously. 'It's so wonderful to see you, especially after we thought we'd lost you.'

Jane swallowed the lump in her throat. 'It's lovely to see you,' she replied warmly.

Noting the tears in his wife's eyes, Tom turned to Jane, teasing wryly, 'You can see I've been ill-treating her!'

'Oh, Tom!' Beth exclaimed remorsefully, then laughed as she saw his face, gentle with love.

'Come on, girls,' kissing Jane's cheek, he gathered up her one bag with raised brows. 'Did you intend to go back this evening?'

It was all lighthearted fun. Jane felt the happiness and love surrounding her two friends like an aura, and while it did accentuate the bleakness of her own future, she was glad she had come. Although her visit must be brief she found just being with them reassuring.

They had a large house, over a mile along the shore. It had been offered to them ready furnished and she could understand the contentment and pride which Beth didn't try and hide.

Tom, unfortunately, had to go out again as soon as they got in, but he promised he wouldn't be late for dinner.

'He works terribly hard,' Beth said proudly after he had kissed her goodbye—a protracted operation, Jane had noticed. It wasn't difficult to see how much they adored each other. Tom might be a big, tough oil man, but he was clearly enslaved by his charming young wife.

'You must have left in a hurry.' Beth, her face still slightly flushed, insisted on making a cup of tea before she took Jane upstairs. 'It seems like a miracle having you here when you could only have got my letter on Friday at the soonest.'

'Yes, on Friday.' Jane let her eyes wander appreciatively about the large, warm kitchen, and as Beth popped the kettle on, she told her about Mrs Frey and France. She didn't mention that she had reasons of her own for coming and had been desperate to leave London.

'It's strange, isn't it,' Beth mused, busy with tea-cups, 'if it hadn't been for this Mrs Frey's misfortune you mightn't have been able to come. I've been longing to see you for weeks, not just because I get sick,' she confessed. 'I admit,' she went on rather guiltily, 'I put that in my letter, believing it might bring you, if nothing else could, but I had no great hopes, considering how tied up you seem to be.'

'Tied up?' queried Jane.

'Your new job!'

'Oh,' it was Jane's turn to flush, then she went white

as she suddenly thought of Paul and didn't want to talk about her job, as it was so involved with him. 'I'm not as busy as all that,' she said haltingly. 'It's just because I'm under contract that I find it difficult to get away.'

'The firm you work for, International—Tom says it's big. Do you know the people who run it?' Beth asked casually.

Unaware that her eyes held a revealingly hunted expression, Jane shrugged aside Beth's seemingly innocent query. 'Beth,' she exclaimed with determination, 'I didn't come all the way here to talk about myself. I promise to tell you about my accident and new job later, but first I want to hear all about you.'

Beth didn't ask Jane what was wrong until they were having elevenses together the following morning, after Tom had gone. Refusing to be put off any longer by Jane's evasive tactics, she spoke frankly.

'I know what's the matter with me,' she said wryly, 'but I'm not sure about you.'

Jane flinched painfully. 'There's nothing wrong . . .'

'At a guess,' Beth interrupted firmly, noting Jane trembling, 'you're either working too hard or you're in love! Ah!' she exclaimed, as colour crept betrayingly to Jane's pale cheeks, 'so that's it, is it? Do you want to talk about it?' she asked, her voice gentler.

Helplessly, Jane shook her head. Beth had always been able to see more than she should. With anguish in her eyes she stared at her. 'There's nothing to talk about, really!'

Beth sighed impatiently. 'Married?'

'No,' unhappily, Jane stopped trying to deviate. 'He's engaged, though.'

'I see.' Beth hesitated. 'Has he any idea how you feel about him?'

'I hope not.' Jane bit her lip, then allowed bitterly, 'Perhaps he has, but it's all so hopeless. He certainly doesn't love me!'

'So,' Beth pondered thoughtfully, 'this is partly,

anyway, why you're here? You haven't told me who he is, but you're running away from him?'

With a smothered cry of misery, Jane tried to deny it, but suddenly everything came tumbling out. She only held back on the more intimate details of their relationship, revealing more of her own involvement than Paul's.

Beth's gentle brown eyes softened compassionately. 'It must have been a terrible shock discovering he had a fiancée.'

'Yes,' Jane whispered, still feeling the pain, 'but it's my own fault. I should have realised I meant nothing to him. He told me often enough.'

'It's funny that he should be the brother of the man you were supposed to have been married to,' Beth reflected slowly.

'He helped me a lot when I was in hospital. I don't know what I should have done without him, he was so kind.'

'All the same,' Beth frowned, 'I can't help feeling he's been a bit unfair.'

'Well, it's over now,' Jane said flatly. She looked at Beth with new resolution suddenly in her eyes. 'After a few days with you and Tom, after I go back, I'm really going to try and believe it.'

By unspoken agreement, during the next two days Paul wasn't mentioned, and because she sensed that Beth felt guilty over her own happiness, Jane made a determined attempt to be cheerful. If occasionally she caught Beth and Tom glancing at her anxiously, she pretended not to notice.

She gave Beth a hand around the house and went for long walks when Tom was there to keep his wife company. To their shared delight, some different pills her doctor had given Beth began to work and she no longer suffered so severely from morning sickness. Jane felt so pleased for her friend she could have wept with relief.

On Wednesday afternoon she walked for miles trying to exhaust herself in the hope of getting a good night's sleep, instead of lying awake for hours thinking of Paul. She must have been more tired than she had imagined, for the following morning she slept in. She was quite startled when Beth woke her, to tell her it was ten o'clock and that Tom was taking her to have coffee with a friend.

'He has the morning off,' Beth smiled. 'I could have left a note, but I wasn't sure if you would find it. See you eat a good breakfast. We'll be back for lunch.'

Jane stayed where she was a few minutes after Beth had gone, listening to Tom's car starting up and the sound of their departure. Beth had looked sweet and so pretty—but surely very excited over a mere cup of coffee? Jane frowned. Perhaps it was because Beth hadn't been out for a while. This might account for the peculiar air of nervousness which had seemed to radiate from her, but for the life of her Jane couldn't think what she had to be nervous about, not with Tom there, ever ready to protect her.

She signed lethargically and turned over, then suddenly she felt the hairs begin to prickle at the back of her head. Apprehensively she realised there were footsteps coming up the stairs. She could have sworn Tom's car had gone but he had obviously forgotten something. Reaching for her dressing-gown, she was just about to jump out of bed and ask if there was anything wrong, when, to her horrified amazement, her bedroom door flew open and Paul walked in. He came right up to the bed and stood looking down at her.

She wasn't sure if she actually fainted, but the room did swing round and she clutched at the sheets in a state of collapse. 'Paul!' his name fell from her lips in a strangled whisper, her eyes dilating with shock as she tried to focus on him. 'How did you get here?'

'More or less the same way as you did, I imagine,' he rasped, his eyes glittering with a mixture of

frustration and anger as they met hers. 'It probably
cost me more.'

What on earth did he mean? Again the room went
dark as she struggled for breath. Blindly she shook her
head, attempting to clear it. He was the last person she
had expected to see. Surely she was still dreaming?

She felt his hands on her shoulders, none too
gently. 'Don't dare pass out on me!' she heard him
snap between clenched teeth. 'Unless it's your
condition?'

'My—condition?'

'Yes,' he bit back, 'I know all about that, it's one of
the reasons I had to see you.'

She still had no idea what he was talking about, but
as her eyes opened slowly to move over his face, she
knew she was hungry for the sight of him. He appeared
grim and tired, the skin round his eyes and mouth
grooved with deep lines. There was a look of suffering
about him which she didn't understand, because it
might have been as great as her own.

'How did you get in?' she breathed, her thoughts
jumping dizzily. 'Beth and Tom . . .'

'I've seen them,' he cut in roughly. 'I arrived before
nine o'clock. I asked for a chance to speak to you alone
and they agreed.'

'They had no right!' she said weakly, shrinking
defensively against her pillows, wishing she could sink
through them or become invisible.

Her few protesting words ignited a flare of anger.
'For God's sake, Jane,' he snapped, 'can't you think of
anything better to say? Surely we're past that stage!'

As she blinked dazedly, he thrust his hands in the
pockets of his well-fitting jeans, as though he didn't
trust them anywhere else. The dark shirt he wore was
tucked into them but open at the neck, revealing the
arrogant strength of his head and shoulders. Jane
swallowed, the beat of her heart increasing rapidly as
she tried to hide how deeply he was able to affect her.

'You still haven't told me why you're here,' she reminded him.

'I'm going to,' he retorted grimly. 'Although I'm sure you must have guessed!'

Bleakly, finding it impossible to believe that anything could have changed between them, Jane whispered, 'No.'

'It beats me,' he said harshly, 'how you can lie there and say that!'

'But I really don't understand!'

'You haven't tried to, have you?' he muttered, sinking down beside her. 'I've been asking you to listen for weeks!'

She wished he hadn't sat there, so close she could feel his furious breath on her face. 'You haven't tried very hard.'

'Don't remind me.' His hard mouth twisted. 'I was determined to have it out with you, so we could put all our stupid bickering, antagonism—call it what you like, behind us, but every time I got near you, you either did or said something that maddened me, and I kept saying—what the hell!'

Jane wanted him to slow down, not only to explain but to be more explicit. She couldn't follow him. Her voice shaking, she said, 'But you're engaged to Leonora!'

'Correction,' he grated, 'Leonora is engaged to my brother.'

Jane's face went as white as her pillows. 'Mark? No, it's not possible. Is this some silly joke?'

'It was,' he confessed grimly, staring into her incredulous eyes. 'Jane, do you really believe I could marry someone like Leonora? She's a nice enough girl, but she'd drive me crazy with her silly chatter within days.'

Jane still couldn't take it in. 'What about last weekend?' she whispered. 'Your parents—everyone . . .'

'Last weekend,' he said dryly, 'it wasn't exactly my

mother's fault that you wouldn't listen. She was trying to tell you Leonora was engaged to Mark, but you said you knew. Unfortunately I was the only one who knew you'd got hold of the wrong man. I waited all weekend for you to discover the mistake you'd made, but amazingly you never did. And when I dragged you off to your room to tell you another fiasco blew up in our faces, and the situation just seemed to get steadily worse from then on.'

'But before that,' she breathed, her face hot as she tried not remember how she had felt in Paul's arms, 'I got the impression . . .'

'Jane,' he said tersely, 'it was entirely my fault that you misunderstood. Mark was going to announce his engagement to Leonora before he went abroad and he would only consent to go if I agreed to keep an eye on her until he returned.'

'Was she the blonde you once said he was out with?' Jane asked uncertainly.

'Yes,' Paul nodded grimly. 'And I did meet her in Paris, before you remember that as well, but it was years ago and she wasn't with me.'

'I don't know how I could have made such a mistake.' Jane was torn by self-impatience and pain, 'What a fool I've been!'

'I should have made a greater effort to clear everything up before I went away,' he said tightly. 'It was something I should have done long before Saturday night, but every time I caught you with one of my staff, to say nothing of Jon Grice, some devil inside me assured me that it would do you no harm to feel jealous for a change. I'd had a surfeit of it, and it can twist a man's soul.'

Jane knew she should be reading between the lines of what he was telling her, but her mind refused to function. 'Last weekend . . .' she began haltingly.

There was a wintry look in his eyes as they rested on her bewildered face. 'Another mistake. When I said I wasn't going to Coombe Park with you, I was deliberately deceiving you, because I meant to be there. By myself, though, not with Leonora. I was furious when my mother rang me on Saturday morning to say Mark had been in touch, announcing his engagement, and asking me to pick Leonora up. To my own credit,' he smiled humourlessly, 'I thought it might be one way of clearing the air, so to speak, between the two of us— until just about everything started going wrong.'

'I must have been blind,' Jane whispered, 'but I was so unhappy, and when you went away it all seemed worse.'

'That was Mark again,' he said curtly. 'Bad trouble in New York. It took until Tuesday morning to sort out, but I realised after I came back that you had plenty of troubles of your own.'

'I suppose I had,' she agreed bleakly.

Paul stared at her, a brief flash of bitterness in his eyes making her feel very cold. As she shivered, he said harshly, 'You don't have to worry if the other man doesn't want to marry you, Jane. I'm going to.'

Jane drew a sharp breath of confusion. 'Paul,' she whispered, 'what on earth are you talking about?'

'It might have set me back,' he muttered, 'when I learned I wouldn't be the first, but I'll make damned sure I'm the last!'

Why was he so angry? Now he wasn't trying to hide it, and she thought she had never seen such a blaze of emotion in a man's face before. Suddenly she knew he wanted her, but that she had done something far worse than any of the previous crimes he had accused her of.

She opened her mouth to implore him to explain, but before she could he caught her close and his lips descended on hers in a savage kiss which she sensed he believed should explain everything. She was trembling before he lifted his head and humiliatingly aware that no matter how he treated her it made no difference to the way she loved him.

'I'm sorry,' he said thickly, levering himself from her a few inches without releasing her, 'I shouldn't have kissed you like that, but you don't know how I felt when I returned to London and couldn't find you anywhere. Mrs Frey, when I caught up with her, could only tell me that she'd given you the week off, and when I went to see if my mother knew anything, I felt worse than ever.'

Jane didn't want to talk about Mrs Denyer, much as she loved her, there seemed other far more important things. She was never quite sure what made her ask, 'What did she say?'

Paul actually swallowed and his face tightened. 'It was more of an attack.' He hesitated, eyes burning. 'She accused me of getting you pregnant.'

'Oh, no!' Jane gasped, dumbfounded as she realised what must have happened. 'Oh, no!' she repeated incredulously.

Taking no notice of the anguish in her eyes, his hands bit into her shoulders painfully. 'You don't have to look so guilty,' he said furiously. 'I know it wasn't me, but I wasn't going to tell her that! I told her it was nobody's damned business but our own and we were going to be married.'

Jane's control almost snapped and to her horror tears threatened. 'You would marry me, knowing I'd had a serious affair with another man?'

'It's happened before,' he said grimly. 'I intend taking care of both you and the child. If,' his voice husked, 'your lover wants either of you, he'll have to kill me first!'

'Oh, Paul!' Jane whispered, no longer trying to hide her eyes were swimming with tears. 'It's Beth who's pregnant—I was asking your mother's advice for her. I did say a friend.'

His face went curiously taut. 'She mentioned that, but she thought it was the usual excuse.'

'No, it wasn't. You'd gone, and I felt dreadful, I just

wanted to return to my flat. I was leaving when I suddenly remembered Beth's morning sickness, but Leonora turned up while I was talking to your mother and I decided to leave it. I had no idea she'd got the wrong impression.'

Paul's mouth moved, but when he didn't say anything Jane panicked. 'I've never belonged to any man,' he cried wildly, 'not even you, yet. You only have one part of me . . .'

Immediately she wished she could have withdrawn that last statement, but even as she flushed in confusion, Paul pounced like an eagle.

'What—part?'

He didn't allow her time to deviate, and suddenly she didn't care any more. She was unlikely to see him after this, anyway. 'My heart,' she muttered miserably, forcing a careless laugh. 'That sounds like a line from an old-fashioned melodrama, doesn't it?'

'You mean—you love me?' His voice was so thick as to be scarcely recognisable. 'Jane!'

'Yes,' she confessed, 'but I know you don't love me.'

'What more do I have to do,' he groaned, catching her close again, 'to prove how much?'

'Paul, please!'

'Be quiet!' His arms enfolded her, bearing her slight body back against the pillows, covering it with his hard form. As his mouth crushed hers, parting her lips with an urgency she couldn't deny, Jane felt she was drowning. She clung to him helplessly, and when he thrust the bedclothes aside to let his arms surround her waist and hips, she let him mould her limbs to his, trembling beneath his undisguised need.

His lips caressed her cheeks and throat, trailing a path of fire down its creamy length to the soft cleft between her breasts. He pushed the delicate lace of her nightgown aside to reveal a rose-petalled tip. His mouth was rapacious and she clutched his muscular arms convulsively in an attempt to regain the last of her willpower which was fast slipping away.

'I love you,' he muttered hoarsely, sensing the shock running through her and trying to reassure her. 'Don't fight me, Jane. The time for fighting is past. Just give in.'

His hand cupped her breasts, strong and caressing, and she closed her eyes as waves of pulsating sensation rushed over her. She began responding passionately, her own hands exploring his neck and shoulders, pressing fiercely against the back of his head as he went on kissing her.

Her fingers tangled in his dark hair as a low moan of surrender escaped her. She felt her body arching against him, aching with a longing demanding satisfaction. Her burning face buried in the strong column of his neck, she begged him to take her.

Reluctantly, as her softly gasping words reached him, Paul drew back. 'If I do, my mother might have just cause for complaint!'

'Would you care?' she cried recklessly, impatient to belong to him completely.

'No,' he said thickly, his face burning dark red, 'I would not.'

'Then . . .?' she whispered huskily, but on a suddenly shortened breath.

'Ah!' his mouth quirked slightly. 'You feel threatened, despite your brave words? Well, let me tell you,' he murmured, 'I intend doing more than that, but first we must talk some more. After we've finished, and you've remembered the way I've treated you, if you still feel you love me, we can take it from there. Only my way's going to be a wedding ring and a short ceremony, whatever you decide!'

'You don't have to marry me.' Jane felt she had been plunged straight into icy seas. 'You told your mother but you were only trying to protect me. I would never hold you to that.'

'That's not what I'm talking about,' he said harshly.

'I've wanted to marry you for a long time. It has nothing to do with my mother's misconceived notions. For both our sakes, Jane, you have to decide if you'll ever be able to forget how much I doubted you. I made your life hell with my terrible accusations, and I don't see how you can ever forgive me.'

'I always forgave you,' she said softly, her blue eyes resting anxiously on the dark agony in his. 'Always, deep down inside me, I understood. And don't you see,' her voice faltered, 'by coming here and asking me to marry you when you believed I'd given myself to another man, you seem to have cancelled everything else out.'

'But it doesn't prove that I trust you.'

'Yes, it does.' She put a gentle hand on his face as if attempting to remove some of the bleakness she saw there. 'Paul darling, haven't I just said, I completely understand. To begin with there were so many difficulties, so many pitfalls in a relationship very new and vulnerable. Everyone's human. I don't believe there's anyone in your position who wouldn't have had some doubts.'

'Oh, God!' He turned his mouth to her caressing palm, burying it in her warm skin deeply, 'If only you knew what I went through because of you! The day before the crash when Colin rang up he was desperate, the things he told me about his wife wouldn't bear repeating. When I got to know you in hospital I had to keep reminding myself, because you seemed so different. I despised myself because I thought my growing desire for you was making me blind.

'That was why I tried to keep my distance. Then after the trip I made to Italy, when I was given indisputable proof, both verbally and from photographs, that you weren't Colin's bigamous wife, I was forced to conclude, because you wore his rings, that you'd somehow grasped a terrible opportunity and decided to pretend you were my brother's wife in order to gain by it.

'Your doctor warned me against confronting you and you know what happened next, but that night you ran from my flat was the worst in my life. I'm not sure yet how I restrained myself from running after you. Where did you go?' he asked grimly. 'Was it really to your old room?'

'I spent the night in a hostel, eventually,' she confessed. 'I learned that Beth had married and was living here and Pat, my other flatmate, had taken in her boy-friend, Jack Adams, so I couldn't stay there.'

With a remorseful groan, Paul tightened his arms round her. 'I accused you of having an affair with him, without any real grounds.'

'Never mind,' she whispered, and for a few moments there was silence between them, then, as though the words were being dragged out of him, Paul went on.

'When I discovered afterwards the real truth about the rings, it still didn't seem to help, although for reasons I still refused to face, I moved heaven and earth to try and find you. When I returned from abroad and found you working on the Frey account it took me quite five minutes to get hold of myself. My poor secretary thought I was suffering from jet-lag!'

'And you were still suspicious,' she reminded him wryly.

'And how!' he agreed grimly. 'It wasn't until I acknowledged that the battle going on inside me had nothing to do with my poor brother or anything else but my own feelings that I understood how I'd been using suspicion, jealousy, distrust—the lot, as a pathetic kind of shield.'

'Shield?' Jane queried.

'To protect myself from admitting I'd fallen in love. That I was committed to the words of the marriage ceremony—forsaking all other, before I'd ever got near a church. I haven't been able to look at another woman since I met you. Sometimes I could have killed you. I began to believe you'd inflicted me with some terrible disease.'

'Sometimes I wished I could!' she said fiercely. Then suddenly she was laughing and so was he. They were laughing and crying, at least she was, though she felt sure there was a betraying dampness on Paul's hard cheek. His arms were tight around her and it was difficult to tell, but she sensed he was as moved as she was.

'I love you,' she whispered, as their laughter stilled and the familiar tension began invading their starved bodies. 'I seem to have loved you for so long . . .'

'I daren't begin telling you how I feel,' he growled, 'or we'll still be here when your friends return.'

'They're married.' Jane enticed him shamelessly by kissing his mouth and letting her hands wander wantonly beneath his shirt, over his hair-roughened chest. 'We wouldn't shock them.'

'I might just manage too,' he murmured, a wicked glint in his eye as he turned the tables on her nicely by slipping out of his shirt and removing the leather belt from his pants. As he caught her to him again, she gasped with alarm, her pulses throbbing wildly.

Then, as he cradled her closely, and his mouth teased the startled impression of her own, she heard him mutter, with gentle mockery, 'I'm going to take a shower, in a few minutes.'

A great sense of happiness filled her and she relaxed, closing her eyes, savouring the feeling of having his hard, masculine body so near her own, all the pain and frustration of the past weeks gone. Her lips parted under his passionately and the gentleness of his kiss changed to a sensual, mind-spinning exploration that left her breathless. Utterly responsive, as his arms tightened, her body trembled with feelings she no longer tried to control. Paul groaned, his eyes darkening to slate grey as he sensuously caressed her, igniting savage flames which might instantly have consumed them, if, with a smothered exclamation, he hadn't suddenly released her and rolled away.

Jane's eyes had gone hazy, but her voice held a mixture of disappointment and pleading as she whispered his name. 'Where are you going?' she breathed, as he got to his feet and towered above her.

'To have a shower, I think,' he said thickly, bending to pick up his discarded shirt. 'Even you must see it wouldn't have been possible in a few more seconds!'

Flushing, Jane came slowly to her senses, her flush deepening as she recalled the hardness of his limbs. 'Beth and Tom might soon be home,' she gulped.

'I've been trying to tell you,' he viewed the colour in her face wryly, 'I want your friends' opinion of me to get better, not worse, and I've waited so long, I guess another two days won't hurt me.'

'Two days?' He was devouring her with his eyes, but keeping his distance, and she didn't understand.

'Before I hired a plane to bring me here,' he explained soberly, 'I saw about a special licence. In two days' time you'll be my wife.'

He hadn't actually asked her, but she decided it wasn't necessary to worry over a small detail like that! Her face glowed with an inner radiance that drew him immediately back to her side.

'Do you like the idea of being my wife?' he asked huskily.

'Oh, yes, Paul, please!' she breathed tremulously. 'I love you.'

He had flames in his eyes as he lifted her hands and pressed his mouth in turn to the centre of each soft palm. 'I love you too,' he murmured thickly. 'I don't know what I would have done if I hadn't found you.'

'How did you?' She was suddenly curious.

'Your friend Pat again,' he said grimly, his voice still rough with pain. 'She knew where Beth was and suggested you might be here. I hope you won't mind leaving again soon?'

'How soon?'

'In the morning.' He was his old self again, giving orders, but Jane didn't mind. She loved him too much to want to change him. He went on, 'You can be married from Coombe Park, my mother would never forgive me otherwise, and you can tell her all about Beth.'

Jane nodded happily, then said slowly, 'Beth's going to be disappointed.'

Paul said gently, 'If she can't get down for the wedding she can come and stay with us later. Her husband, too, if he can make it.'

'She'll love that,' Jane replied, leaning forward to press a grateful little kiss on his lean cheek. 'You said you were going to Australia,' she reminded him uncertainly.

'I've arranged for someone else to go,' he replied. 'I'm going to steal you from Olive Frey for another two weeks. After we're married we'll go the South of France—I have a cottage there I'm sure you'll love. Later on, I intend taking you to Australia on a prolonged honeymoon. That is, if you've got over your fear of flying?'

'I have,' she assured him, her heart beating with joy at the thought of sharing any kind of future with him. 'Coming from Glasgow,' she confessed, 'I had my doubts, but I was so miserable over you that I think, in a strange way, this helped me over the worst of it. Anyway,' she smiled gently at him, 'I was all right.'

'You don't know what I went through,' Paul muttered tensely, 'at the thought of you being terrified of flying here and not being near to be able to help you.'

'I was only terrified of an empty future,' she admitted unevenly. 'I loved you so much and couldn't stop thinking about you, for all I believed you were committed to another girl.'

'Oh, my darling!' He released her hands and drew her close, no longer able to resist it. 'I've been despicable,' his eyes were dark with remorse, 'but I'll make it up to you, I promise. When we're married, I'll even let you go on working, if you like.'

He spoke with a meekness so out of character, she couldn't help smiling. 'I'd rather just be your wife,' she whispered, her cheeks flushing as their eyes met, revealing their mutual desire and the amusement faded from her face.

'Oh, my darling!' Paul said again, his mouth seeking hers in a kiss which was an act of possession more compelling than anything they had shared before. 'You'll never regret it,' he promised against her trembling lips.

As his arms tightened, she gave herself up to him without reserve, meeting the flame of his passion with her own, her pulses racing as she felt his hard body shake in response. Now they were together, at last, she knew this was love for ever, exactly the way she wanted it to be.

ROMANCE

Variety is the spice of romance

Each month, Mills and Boon publish new romances. New stories about people falling in love. A world of variety in romance – from the best writers in the romantic world. Choose from these titles in February.

NEVER TRUST A STRANGER Kay Thorpe
COME LOVE ME Lilian Peake
CASTLE OF THE LION Margaret Rome
SIROCCO Anne Mather
TANGLE OF TORMENT Emma Darcy
A MISTAKE IN IDENTITY Sandra Field
RIDE THE WIND Yvonne Whittal
BACKFIRE Sally Wentworth
A RULING PASSION Daphne Clair
THE SILVER FLAME Margaret Pargeter
THE DUKE WORE JEANS Kay Clifford
THE PRICE OF FREEDOM Alison Fraser

On sale where you buy paperbacks. If you require further information or have any difficulty obtaining them, write to: Mills & Boon Reader Service, PO Box 236, Thornton Road, Croydon, Surrey CR9 3RU, England.

Mills & Boon
the rose of romance

4 BOOKS FREE

Enjoy a Wonderful World of Romance...

Passionate and intriguing, sensual and exciting. A top quality selection of four Mills & Boon titles written by leading authors of Romantic fiction can be delivered direct to your door absolutely **FREE**!

Try these Four Free books as your introduction to Mills & Boon Reader Service. You can be among the thousands of women who enjoy six brand new Romances every month PLUS a whole range of special benefits.

- Personal membership card.

- Free monthly newsletter packed with recipes, competitions, exclusive book offers and a monthly guide to the stars.

- Plus extra bargain offers and big cash savings.

There is no commitment whatsoever, no hidden extra charges and your first parcel of four books is absolutely FREE!

Why not send for more details now? Simply complete and send the coupon to MILLS & BOON READER SERVICE, P.O. BOX 236, THORNTON ROAD, CROYDON, SURREY, CR9 3RU, ENGLAND. OR why not telephone us on 01-684 2141 and we will send you details about the Mills & Boon Reader Service Subscription Scheme — you'll soon be able to join us in a wonderful world of Romance.

Please note:— **READERS IN SOUTH AFRICA** write to Mills & Boon Ltd., Postbag X3010, Randburg 2125, S. Africa.

Please send me details of the Mills & Boon Reader Service Subscription Scheme.

NAME (Mrs/Miss) _____ EP6

ADDRESS _____

_____

COUNTY/COUNTRY _____

POSTCODE _____

BLOCK LETTERS PLEASE